# THE RACE
# AGAINST TIME

# BERNARD PALMER

Tyndale House
Publishers, Inc.
Wheaton, Illinois

*Bernard Palmer is also the well-known author of the Breck
Western Series and* My Son, My Son. *He lives with his wife,
Marjorie, in Holdrege, Nebraska.*

Previously published by Moody Press under the title
*Danny Orlis and the Boy Who Would Not Listen.*

First Tyndale House printing, February 1989
Library of Congress Catalog Card Number 88-51653
ISBN 0-8423-0560-2
© 1957 by Bernard Palmer
Printed in the United States of America

# Contents

# ONE
## *Mrs. Barber's problem*

Danny Orlis left the school house in Cedarton and walked along the darkened street toward home. It was only four o'clock, but the sun had already been chased behind the horizon, and the little town was clothed in the soothing shades of night. A car crept up the icy street ahead of him, its headlights making the snow glisten.

Mrs. Barber would be home probably and have supper ready. At least he hoped she would. Man, but a guy got hungry playing hockey.

Mrs. Barber was not home, however. Her son, Kirk, and a strange man were sitting in the living room talking.

"Good afternoon, young man," the man said, getting to his feet. "I've been waiting to talk to your mother. When I heard you at the door I thought she was returning."

"He's not my brother," Kirk said briskly. "He just lives here."

Self-consciously Danny grinned.

"My name is Meyer," the man went on. "I came to take another look at the house. I'm really very interested in it. It's not a new house, but it's solidly built and has plenty of room. I've looked at a number of homes here, but this one really takes my eye."

Danny said nothing, but he sighed deeply. He could not blame the guy who owned the house for wanting to sell it, but what were Mrs. Barber and Kirk and Karen going to do? There was not another house for rent in Cedarton that they could afford.

Mr. Meyer was eyeing him critically.

"When do you think she'll be back?" he asked.

"She ought to be home before long. We usually eat quite early."

Mr. Meyer took his watch from his pocket again and frowned as he glanced at it. "I'm afraid I won't be able to wait. I've got another appointment uptown, and I'm already late for it. Would you tell her that I stopped and that I'll be back again in a couple of days?"

"Sure thing."

With an almost imperceptible toss of his head, Mr. Meyer indicated that he wanted Danny to follow him to the door. When they were out of Kirk's hearing the stranger turned to him.

"I'm going to ask you a personal question, young fellow, and you don't have to answer it if you'd rather not. I've been wondering about Mrs. Barber. How does she manage to take care of herself and the children? Does she have a private income?"

"Only the magazine business," Danny told him, "and what little I pay for board and room. It's awfully hard for her."

"I can imagine that." He looked at Danny seriously.

Mr. Meyer had his hand on the doorknob before he turned back. "Tell me," he said, "which do you play—football or hockey?"

"Right now it's hockey."

"I thought so. I could tell by looking at you. You have the build for it."

Danny grinned in spite of himself.

"I've got a boy who plays hockey for Edgerton. He must be about your age."

"You haven't!" Danny echoed. Meyer! Ken Meyer! Who didn't know Ken Meyer, the handsome, conceited league-leading scorer for the season?

"I played against him a while back. Will he be coming here soon? We could sure use him."

Mr. Meyer shook his head. "I wish he would be coming when I move. But the coach wants him to stay and finish the season with them."

And with that, Mr. Meyer pulled on his coat and went out into the February night.

Kirk came around the hall doorway.

"Is that dope, Ken Meyer, going to move to Cedarton?" he demanded.

"He's a good hockey player," Danny said. "I wish we were getting him to help us in the tournament."

"Yeah," Kirk said without enthusiasm, "he's a good hockey player, all right. But the trouble is that he knows it. And he's a contemptible player, Danny. You remember how he tripped you when the referee wasn't watching."

Mrs. Barber came in just then, and Danny told her about Mr. Meyer.

"Did he say anything about the house?" she asked

quickly, her eyes betraying her concern. "Did he act like he's interested in it?"

"I'm afraid he is," Danny answered reluctantly. "He said that he'd looked at a lot of houses here in town, but he hadn't found anything that he liked half as well. He's coming back again as soon as he can."

The color drained from her face. "I've looked at a good many houses, too," she said wearily. "That's what I've been doing all afternoon. I've gone from one realtor to another, but they all gave me the same story." She swallowed hard and dabbed furtively at her eyes with the corner of her handkerchief.

"It isn't as if we can afford to pay high rent. We could get any of several places if it didn't matter what they cost."

Mrs. Barber sat down wearily and bit her lip. "I know that God cares," she said. She was talking more to herself than to Danny, "but it would be awfully easy to get to thinking that he doesn't."

Danny went up to bed at the usual time that evening, but he could not sleep for thinking about Mrs. Barber. What would happen to her now?

She did not talk about money matters much, but he knew that she was having a hard time getting by as it was. Once in a while she would have to let a grocery bill go for a week or so, and every now and then she would not be able to pay her light bill in time to get the discount. What was she going to do? For a time he prayed for her.

# TWO
## *Playing with trouble*

Some time after eleven o'clock, the wind came up and howled under the eaves and shrieked through the pines just outside the window. Danny got up to look out, shivering in the cold. The ice was so thick on the glass that he could not see whether it was snowing or not.

The following morning when he got up, however, he saw that the sidewalks and streets were choked with drifts. Fine, new snow was still swirling down.

"There won't be any school today," Kirk chirped gaily as he saw Danny on the stairs. "I just heard it on the radio. No school today. It's snowing too hard to go to school."

The Orlis boy grinned at him. Somehow Kirk reminded him of his brother, Ron, at home. "What are you going to do?"

"As soon as I eat breakfast, Pete and I are going to get a bunch of kids together over in his yard."

"I thought you said it was snowing too hard to go to school."

"This is different," Kirk answered.

11

Along in the middle of the morning it quit snowing. At noon Danny plowed through the drifts to school. They were not holding classes, and only a small handful of children ventured out, but he had some studying to do.

Kay Milburn came into the library and sat down beside him. Her blond curls were blown attractively about her small oval face and her eyes were dancing.

"Hi, Danny."

He ran his fingers self-consciously through his own crop of sandy hair, and wondered whether his tie was straight.

"I thought you'd be home by the fire, shivering," he told her. "This is a little different than Mexico."

"I'm getting to be a regular Eskimo," she answered. Then she leaned forward and lowered her voice: "I'm so happy I could cry, Danny. I think I've got Marilyn Forester to go to Bible club with me."

"You have!" he exclaimed. That was something they had been praying about for weeks.

"At least she promised that she'd go with me tonight," Kay went on excitedly. "Oh, Danny, pray that she won't change her mind!"

At the last minute Marilyn tried to wriggle out of it, but Kay talked her into going.

"It only lasts an hour."

"I know, but I've got a lot of studying to do."

"We can study together when we get home. You'll like it, Marilyn. I know you will."

"Well," she said reluctantly. "I guess I could go this once to see what it's like."

Kay's face brightened.

"But don't get the idea that I'm joining anything.

I'm just going because you've asked me so many times."

There were thirty or forty high school kids out for Bible club that night, but it seemed as though the lesson was meant for Marilyn. The leader spoke on Nicodemus. He explained in simple words how a person must confess that he is a sinner and put his trust in the Lord Jesus if he wants to have eternal life.

Kay looked over at the girl she had brought with her. Marilyn squirmed uncomfortably, and sighed in relief when the meeting was over. She got her coat and hurried into the hall where she stood waiting for Kay.

"I'm supposed to stay for an officers' meeting," Kay said, "but I talked with Danny and got him to postpone it."

"Don't do that on account of me."

"Oh, but I promised that we'd do our homework together."

By this time they were out of the church and were heading up the sidewalk toward the Forester home. Kay looked at her companion hopefully.

"It was a nice meeting, wasn't it?"

"If you go for that stuff I guess it was all right," Marilyn retorted. "But I don't think I'd be interested in going again. I want to have a little excitement. Some fun!"

Nevertheless she pushed her lessons aside when they were alone together up in her room, and for almost an hour asked Kay questions about the Bible and the "new birth." They were pointed, searching questions that showed she had been thinking deeply.

When at last they finished their lessons and Kay

got up to leave, Marilyn followed her down into the living room.

"You know, Kay," she said impulsively, "I wish that you were rooming with us. I already feel as though you're my very best friend. Why don't we walk to school together in the morning?"

"That sounds like fun, but I have to be there at eight o'clock."

"So do I."

They looked at one another and laughed.

For the next ten days or so Kay and Marilyn Forester were inseparable. And, strangely enough, it was Marilyn who took most of the initiative. She called Kay before leaving for school in the morning, and waited for her in the hall almost every afternoon. She surprised Kay by going to church with her, and once she even went to prayer meeting.

Marilyn knew from the very beginning about the missionary from Mexico who was speaking at the Women's Missionary Society on that Thursday afternoon. She was almost as anxious as Kay to go and hear her.

"The thing that makes me so mad," Kay confided, "is that I can't get to see her because she's speaking at Edgemont at a banquet tonight and will be leaving here before school is out."

"She has been down where your mother is, hasn't she?" Marilyn asked.

"Mother wrote that she was coming through here and hoped that I'd get to hear her. They're stationed about one hundred fifty miles apart, but they do get to see each other every once in a while."

"Maybe you can see her at noon," the other girl sympathized.

Kay had thought she would get a chance to see the missionary during the noon hour, and impatiently counted the time until the last morning class was out.

"We'll hurry to my place," Marilyn said breathlessly, "and phone her. You know where she's going here in town, don't you?"

But when they called the number they learned that Miss Davis was not expected until two o'clock.

"And," Mrs. Wisman said, "I'm afraid she won't be here long after the meeting, either. We had a phone call yesterday telling us that she would have to be put on the program so she can leave here by four o'clock."

Kay was heart-sick when she set the phone back on its cradle.

"But you've just got to see her," Marilyn said with firm determination.

Kay was disturbed.

"I've just got to see her," she said, "I—I've been so homesick ever since I found out she's coming through here that I don't know what to do."

Marilyn went over and sat on the divan beside her.

"I've got a notion to go anyway," she said.

"Skip school?" Marilyn echoed. "Old Brown would skin anyone alive for that."

Kay swallowed hard, and for a moment could not say anything. Tears stood full in her eyes.

"It's been six whole months since I've seen Mother, or anyone from down home," she said finally. "It's the longest I've ever been away from home before."

"I've got it!" Marilyn exclaimed, brightening. "Give me that phone book. I'll fix things."

"What are you going to do?"

"I'm going to call the school and tell them you're sick," Marilyn replied. "You've got to get to see her."

"Do you think you should?" Kay asked hesitantly.

"Sure, why not?"

Quickly, before Kay could change her mind, Marilyn dialed the number.

# THREE
## *A white lie*

"I–I don't think we ought, Marilyn," Kay stammered.
"I want to go and hear Miss Davis, but I'm not sick. I
don't want you to lie."

Marilyn cupped her hand over the mouthpiece.

"Don't be silly. I've done this lots of times, in fact,
every time I've been out late and don't want to get up
and go to school in the morning. It's always worked
for me. No one will know the difference."

She turned to the telephone quickly as the school
secretary answered.

"This is Mrs. Barnes," Marilyn said crisply. "I've
called to tell you that Kay Milburn won't be in school
this afternoon. She came home a few minutes ago
with a splitting headache. . . . She stays with us, you
know. Thank you."

Marilyn hung up the phone and turned to her friend
smiling triumphantly.

"There," she announced, "it's all done. And it was a
lot easier than going into the office and trying to con-
vince Mr. Brown that he ought to excuse you from

class this afternoon. You can go hear the missionary and you won't be getting an unexcused absence."

Kay got up and walked nervously across the room. It was the first time she had ever done anything like that.

"We—we've lied to them, Marilyn," she said nervously. "We shouldn't have done that."

"Well," Marilyn replied flippantly, "you would have been sick if you hadn't gotten to go to the church to hear Miss Davis." She got up and started to put on her coat, then stopped suddenly.

"Say," she began, turning toward Kay, "if you'd call out to school for me and tell them that I'm sick I wouldn't have to go this afternoon, either. Then we could both go and hear this missionary friend of your mother's."

"Oh, but I couldn't do that," Kay protested quickly. "I couldn't lie to them that way, Marilyn. It wouldn't be right."

Marilyn snorted her disgust.

"Well, I like that. It was all right for me to lie so you didn't have to go. The least you could do would be to help me out."

Kay shook her head miserably.

Quickly Marilyn got into her coat. "Just wait until you want me to do something for you. I'll remember, Kay Milburn."

The missionary's daughter did not move until after Marilyn had flounced out of the house, leaving her alone. Then she walked back to the chair where she had laid her coat and put it on. Her face was flushed crimson and her lips were trembling.

Marilyn was the one who had done it, she tried,

doggedly, to tell herself. It had been Marilyn's idea in the first place. She had not even given her a chance to think things out. She had gone ahead and called the school, on her own. And besides, she just had to hear Miss Davis. She just had to! It was the only chance she would have to talk with someone who had seen her mother recently. Her heart ached just the same.

Kay walked out of the house and down the brick steps. At the walk she hesitated for a moment, then turned and shuffled dejectedly toward the church. She tried, grimly, to force the nagging thought of what had just been done out of her mind.

The church was across town from where Marilyn lived. By the time Kay got there, the meeting was ready to begin. A slim, graying woman in strange dress was sitting on the platform.

"What's the program today?" Kay whispered to the woman who was sitting next to her.

"Miss Tompkins is going to tell us about her work in Guatemala. I was talking with her a little while ago and she's had some of the most wonderful experiences. I'm so anxious to hear her."

"But—but I thought a missionary from Mexico was going to talk this afternoon," Kay protested weakly.

"She was," the woman affirmed, "but the pastor of the church she spoke in last night called us the first thing this morning and told us that she had been taken ill quite suddenly this morning. We were so fortunate that Miss Tompkins just happened to be visiting in town, and she was gracious to come and speak for us at the last minute."

"I—I see," Kay stammered.

She had let Marilyn Forester lie for her. She had let her tell the school authorities that she was sick, now Miss Davis was not even at the missionary meeting.

In that instant, Kay saw what she had done in all its ugliness. And to think that she had been trying to deal with Marilyn about her soul. What opportunity would she have now to win her friend for the Lord?

Eyes burning with tears, Kay got to her feet and stumbled outside. The raw March wind swirling through the naked trees stung her face. She scarcely felt it as she walked along the sidewalk toward home. She had lied—yes, lied.

Somehow Kay managed to get back quickly to Mrs. Barnes's big, comfortable house. There she threw herself, sobbing across her bed.

# FOUR
## *The hard road back*

Danny Orlis met Marilyn in the corridor after school that afternoon.

"By the way," he said to her, "where was Kay this afternoon? I didn't see her in class."

"She's sick," Marilyn said. A tiny smile flickered on the corners of her lips and she winked at him.

"I saw her this morning, and she certainly didn't look as though anything was wrong. Wonder if she'll be able to be out to Young People's this evening."

"Oh, yes," Marilyn answered, "she'll be well enough to go there."

Danny scratched his head. "I don't get it."

"You see, Kay's just sick enough not to be able to go to school this afternoon," Marilyn said. "That's all."

With that she swept away.

Rick Harris and Butch Winston came up to where Danny was standing.

"Say," Rick began, "we just heard something a little while ago."

Danny faced them.

"Is it true that Ken Meyer is going to move to Cedarton?" Butch blurted.

The Orlis boy nodded. "That's what his dad said. I guess he's coming as soon as the hockey season is over.

"Man, oh, man!" Butch was rubbing his hands together. "We'll really have a power house of a hockey team next year. With him on the ice, no one in the league will be able to hold us."

"He's good, all right," Danny answered.

Rick shook his head. "I've got an uncle over in Edgerton who knows Ken real well. He says that he's a good hockey player but that he's awfully wild. He won't train or anything. I don't think he'd last long with Coach Collins."

"Listen," Winston said, "he's so good that Collins wouldn't *dare* to kick him off the team. I don't care what he did."

"I wouldn't be so sure of that," Danny told him. "I don't think it would make any difference to the coach how good a guy was. If he didn't train, he wouldn't get to play."

The other boy smiled. "You just wait and see."

Kay had been going to go to Young People's with Danny that night, but she called him after supper and told him that she would not be able to. Her eyes were red and swollen. The pain in her heart had increased until she knew that she could not sit through the meeting.

Miserably she got down on her knees and tried to pray, but the words would not come. The Bible said that a person had to be right with God and with other people if prayer was to be answered. And she was not right; her aching heart told her that.

Kay knew, then, what she had to do. She got up, put on her robe, and went down into the living room where Mrs. Barnes was sitting.

"Mrs. Barnes," she began, "I–I have something that I have to tell you."

The kindly Christian woman turned to face her. "Yes, Kay."

"I wasn't in school this afternoon," she blurted. "I wanted to go and hear the missionary at church. It was supposed to be Miss Davis from Mexico. So I had Marilyn call the principal's office and tell them that I was sick. I'm terribly sorry."

"I'm so glad you talked with me, Kay," the older woman said gently.

"I've got to go and talk with them out at school to-morrow. I don't want them to think that I was sick when I wasn't."

"They already know," Mrs. Barnes continued.

The girl looked up quickly, a question in her eyes.

"They thought the voice sounded a little young, so after Marilyn hung up they called me to verify the message. I was just sitting here praying that you would come and tell me about it."

The flood gates broke and Kay sank, sobbing, into a chair across from her landlady.

Mrs. Barnes got up and put her arm about Kay's shoulder. For a long minute she said nothing.

"Now, honey," she began at last, "you know that the Lord is quick to forgive if we come to him in repentance and ask him for forgiveness."

Together they knelt in prayer.

Kay Milburn tried to phone Marilyn later that evening, but her friend was out somewhere. And when she called her the following morning, Marilyn had already gone to school. Kay went directly to the principal's office and asked to see Mr. Brown.

"Well," he began curtly, "what have you got to say for yourself?"

"I want to tell you how sorry I am that I—I lied and skipped school yesterday afternoon," she stammered.

His eyes narrowed. "What did Mrs. Barnes do, tell you that we had called her?"

"She told me," Kay said, "after I went down and—and confessed what I had done."

He looked at her quizzically.

"You see, I'm a Christian," Kay tried to explain, "I know I shouldn't have done it. I knew it at the time. But I wanted to hear the missionary from down in Mexico where Mother is so badly that I—that I—" She swallowed hard, and it was almost a minute before she could go on. "I didn't act like a Christian, Mr. Brown, and I'm so ashamed."

He picked up a pencil and began to toy with it absentmindedly.

"Why did you go to Mrs. Barnes and tell her what you had done?" he asked. "And why did you come here just now?"

Kay was twisting her handkerchief into a tight little knot. "It's because I'm a Christian," she repeated. "And I know that what I did is wrong. So I just had to go to Mrs. Barnes and to you to ask your forgiveness."

"I've been a teacher for twenty-five years," Mr. Brown told her. "This is the first time anything like this has happened to me." He sat down and began to write out a blue slip. "I'm going to give you an excuse for yesterday. If we had more like you in our high school, we would not have so many problems."

She smiled with relief.

"It isn't that I'm any different than any of the others," she told him. "It's only that I'm a Christian, and I'm trying to live the way Christ would have me."

From there she went to each of the classes she had skipped, told the teachers what had happened, and asked their forgiveness.

"Now," she said to herself, "if I can just talk to Marilyn, I'll have this mess straightened out."

But it was not so simple to see her friend. Marilyn was in a club that met after school, and it was not until after dinner that evening that she found her at the ice cream shop. Marilyn was sitting in a booth alone.

"Hi," she said as Kay approached her, "long time no see."

"That's right," Kay said. "I've been trying to call you, though. I want to talk to you."

Marilyn pushed aside the ice cream dish and listened as Kay talked to her.

"And so," she concluded almost tearfully, "I want to ask your forgiveness, too."

"My forgiveness?" Marilyn echoed. "Why should you ask me to forgive you? It was all my idea in the first place. I'm the one who got you into the mess. You don't have to ask me to forgive you."

"But I shouldn't have let you do it," the missionary's daughter said. "I'm a Christian, Marilyn. I should act like one. And I certainly didn't when I let you lie for me."

Marilyn Forester was quiet for a long while.

"Does being a Christian mean that much to you?" she asked hoarsely.

Kay nodded. A tear hung on her eyelash momentarily, then rolled silently down her cheek.

"You know, Kay," Marilyn said huskily, "I've been fighting the Lord for a long while. I've kidded myself into thinking that I'm just as good as you are. But I see now that—that—" she gulped hard. "Kay, tell me again, how does a person become a Christian?"

# FIVE
## *No turning back*

For several seconds Kay and Marilyn sat tensely in the booth staring at one another. The ice cream shop was rapidly becoming a hive of noise, but neither of the girls noticed. Marilyn moistened her lips and leaned forward earnestly.

"You—you mean you want to hear the gospel again?" Kay echoed. It seemed incredulous. "You mean you'll actually listen?"

"You've shown me that I have to become a Christian, Kay," she said huskily. "I've been kidding myself when I've said I didn't need Christ. Explain salvation to me again."

"Of course I will, Marilyn," Kay spoke thankfully. "That's one thing we've been praying about for weeks."

"I know."

A couple of high school friends went by just then and spoke briefly to Marilyn. She answered mechanically without even realizing that she had spoken.

"Rick tried and tried to tell me what it means to be a Christian," she went on. "For a while I was so upset about it I couldn't sleep nights, but I wouldn't listen. Remember that Sunday when he left me in the theater lobby? I didn't stay for the picture either. I went home and. . . ." Her voice trailed away and she worked hard to keep back the tears. "If I hadn't been so proud, I'd have called you and had you come over that very night. I was so miserable."

Kay reached out and laid her hand on Marilyn's. "You can call me any time, Marilyn," she said tenderly. "Any time at all."

As Kay fumbled in her handbag for her Testament she looked about the busy ice cream shop. All the booths were filled with excited, laughing guys and girls, and a growing crowd was gathering in the far corner waiting for space.

*Perhaps it would be better,* she told herself, *if Marilyn and I went where it is quiet.* She stopped short. Did she really want to be alone with Marilyn because it was better that way, or was it because she was ashamed to have anyone know that she was talking to her friend about Christ?

With determination, she took the Testament out of her bag and opened it to the third chapter of John. The color came up into her cheeks as one of the guys standing nearby noticed the Testament and nudged his companion. Her heart was beating faster, but her voice was clear and even as she began to speak.

"I don't know why," she said, "but whenever I get the opportunity to explain salvation to someone I usually use this chapter. I guess it's one of my favorites."

Quietly she read about Nicodemus, how he came to Christ at night to seek answers to questions about Jesus that had troubled him.

"I remember that from the first Bible club meeting," Marilyn said, smiling feebly. "But there are so many things I don't understand."

"There are many things I don't understand either," Kay said. "But the plan of salvation is so clear anyone can understand it." She read verses which explained that everyone had sinned, that the wages of sin is death, and that confessing our sin and putting our trust in Christ is the only way that we may have eternal life.

She paused, unaware that half a dozen guys and girls had crowded near and were listening. "Are you ready to turn your life over to Christ, Marilyn?" she almost whispered.

"Oh boy! This is rich!" one of the guys said laughing raucously. "A revival meeting right here in Owen's Ice Cream Parlor."

"Don't you do it, Marilyn," somebody advised. "It will be the end of all your good times. Besides, we don't want to lose the best dancer in the junior class."

"We wouldn't lose her, pal," the first guy retorted. "She'll just go to lugging a Bible around the dance floor. That's all."

"I'll tell you what you do, Marilyn," Butch Winston exclaimed. "You go right ahead and get saved, or whatever you call it, then come over and try to convert me. How about it?"

Marilyn pushed back her ice cream dish and got to her feet. The color had gone from her face and her lips were set in a thin, tight line.

"I know this, Butch," she said, her voice trembling a little. "We are both sinners and bound for destruction unless we do take Christ as our personal Savior. She swallowed hard. "You can make fun of me all you want to, but I'm going to do just that tonight."

Butch stepped back as though he had been slapped. A tense hush settled over that corner of the ice cream shop. Grins left their faces. Kay got quickly to her feet.

"Come on, Marilyn," she whispered. "Let's leave."

An aisle opened respectfully for them.

"What do you know about that!" Butch said as Marilyn and Kay walked out the door. "If I hadn't seen it, no one could have made me believe it!"

"I wouldn't either," his companion replied. "Marilyn's the last girl in school I'd ever expect to go religious."

When Danny and Rick entered the ice cream shop half an hour or so later, Butch and his friends were still talking about it.

"You ought to have been here, Orlis," Butch said, his voice harsh and taunting. "You'd have been proud of Marilyn. Real proud."

"What are you talking about?" Danny wanted to know. "What gives?"

"She's a religious fanatic," Butch snorted, "just like you and Rick."

"You mean Marilyn Forester testified in here tonight?" Danny echoed. It was hard to believe.

"I don't know whether you call it testifyin' or not," one of the other guys cut in, "but she sure told Butch off. She told him he was going to—"

"Keep still!" Butch cut in shortly.

Rick grasped Danny by the arm.

"Do you suppose Marilyn has really taken Christ as her Savior?" he asked.

"I don't know," Danny replied. "Let's go find out."

They left the ice cream shop hurriedly and drove to Marilyn's home, but the only light in the house was in her bedroom, so they drove on.

"Do you suppose she really did?" Rick asked eagerly.

"Something must have happened to make her talk to Butch like that."

Back at the Forester home, Kay went with Marilyn to her bedroom. Neither of them had spoken since they left the ice cream shop.

"You know," Marilyn said at last, her voice thin and choked. "I feel that I'm a Christian already. I asked Christ to be my Savior right there in the ice cream shop. I knew that I was a sinner and that I had to put all my trust in Jesus for salvation."

Kay's eyes were brimming. "That's wonderful," she said. "And you testified almost at the same time. I don't think I have ever been happier."

Marilyn sat down on the bench before the dressing table and turned toward Kay.

"I'm glad it happened that way," she said. "Now I won't need to worry about letting the gang at school know where I stand."

The missionary's daughter smiled warmly. "That's right."

"I want to wait up for Mother and Daddy, so I can tell them what has happened," Marilyn went on. "Then I want to call Rick and tell him and apologize for treating him like I did."

"That's good," Kay agreed.

Marilyn was silent for a long while.

"You know," she said at last. "This morning, and all

the time before that, I've always thought of Mother and Daddy, with their cocktail parties and dances and country clubbing, as ideal people, the kind I always wanted to be. But now . . ." She stopped and drew her handkerchief across her eyes. "I know now that they're—*they're lost, Kay.* If something happened to one of them, I'd never see them again."

"We'll pray for them, Marilyn," the missionary girl said softly, and they did.

# SIX
## *An uncertain future*

Marilyn was in church and Sunday school the following Sunday morning and at Bible club with Rick on Monday night. The story of her conversion spread like wildfire across the school. Some of the Christians talked with her about it, but others did not dare to mention it.

"After all," Danny overheard one instructor say to another on Monday morning, "Marilyn's the daughter of the most influential couple in town."

The crowd at Bible club was bigger than usual that night. When time came for testimonies Marilyn was the first to rise. Her face was serious and a thin line of perspiration stood out on her forehead.

"I—I know there are guys and girls here tonight who haven't taken Christ as their Savior," she stammered. "I—I just want to tell you that it's *wonderful* to be a Christian."

She stood there for a moment or two, helplessly, then dropped to her seat. Kay reached over and squeezed her hand.

Marilyn's coming out for Christ seemed to spark the other Christians in the Bible club, and the little group began to grow steadily.

"Boy, it seems good to have a bunch like that out for Bible club, doesn't it?" Danny said to Kay as they walked home after the third meeting.

"I'll say," she replied. "It seems as though things have broken loose now that Marilyn has taken a stand for the Lord."

"You can say that again," he answered.

They walked on for a half a block or so. "You know, Danny," Kay said at last. "I'm worried about Marilyn."

"How's that?" he asked.

"Things are so hard for her at home," Kay said. "She told her folks and they think she's out of her mind going for 'religion' that way. They told her if she didn't snap out of it, they wouldn't let her go to our church, or to Bible club, either."

"That's tough. It's hard enough for a new Christian to get both feet on the ground without having opposition at home."

"They've been insisting that she go to shows and dances," Kay went on, "We'll have to pray for her, Danny."

"Yes, we will."

Danny was still thinking about Marilyn and her problems when he entered the Barber house and started up the stairs to his room.

"Danny!" Kirk called from the kitchen. "Is that you?

"Right you are!" Danny sang out.

Kirk appeared in the doorway. His thin, pinched face was ashen and streaked with tears.

"What's the matter, Kirk?" Danny demanded.

34

"What's wrong?" In four steps he was down the steps and in the hall beside the boy. "What's the matter?" he asked again.

"Something terrible has happened!" Kirk managed.

Kirk Barber's breath was coming in quick gasps and the corners of his mouth were twitching nervously. He swallowed hard.

"Something terrible must have happened, Danny," he repeated.

"What is it, Kirk?" Danny demanded. "What's wrong?"

"I–I don't know for sure," he stammered, "but it must be terrible. It's got to be. Mother's in the bedroom crying, just like she did when Daddy died. She won't talk to me."

"Is Karen all right?"

"Sure," the younger boy replied. "I left her at school twenty minutes ago."

"Then it can't be serious," Danny asserted. Still his own heart was hammering a wild tattoo as he flung open the bedroom door. "Mrs. Barber," he exclaimed, "what's wrong?"

He stopped abruptly as she stirred. Kirk moved up beside him, fright still twisting his face. She was lying in the same position as she had been when Kirk came home from school and found her. Her shoulders quivered every now and then, and a muffled sob escaped her lips.

"Mrs. Barber," Danny repeated, "what's the matter?"

She choked off a sob and turned over, her eyes red and swollen.

"What's wrong?" he asked again. "What's happened?"

She sat up slowly and dabbed at her eyes with a tear-soaked handkerchief.

"What happened, Mother?" Kirk broke in anxiously.

"I–I had a phone call. And the house has been sold. We've got to move the first of the month."

"Oh," Danny sighed deeply. "For a couple of minutes I thought it was something important."

"But it is important," she protested. "I've looked for a house or an apartment to rent, and I can't find a thing. There isn't any place in Cedarton where we can move. I don't know what we're going to do."

Kirk sat down on the bed beside her and put his arm awkwardly about her shoulder. She leaned wearily against him.

"You know," the Orlis boy said at last, "my mother and dad have been in some hard spots up at the Angle. There've been times when they didn't know what they should do, and it didn't seem that there was an answer to their problems. But Dad always says that Jesus can carry burdens better than we can."

"I've prayed, Danny." When she spoke her voice was dull and hollow. "You'll never know how hard I've prayed. But it hasn't done any good. We still don't have a place to live, and I just don't have the strength to keep looking."

Danny pulled up a chair beside the bed and sat down.

"How do you know that it hasn't done you any good to pray?" he asked. "We haven't been put out yet."

"No," she said, sniffling, "but in a couple of weeks we're going to have to get out, and we have no place to go."

Danny talked with her for a time, and then the three of them prayed. When Kirk, who was last, finished, Mrs. Barber smiled weakly and got to her feet still dabbing at her eyes.

"I'm sorry I went to pieces," she apologized. "I should have known that God cares what happens to us—that he's going to look after us and provide the things that we need. I feel so much better now."

Kirk smiled at her.

"That's sure right," Danny answered.

Mrs. Barber smiled at Kirk and took hold of his shoulder. "Come on, son," she said. "Let's see if I can find you something to eat."

"That sounds good to me," Kirk replied.

While Mrs. Barber cooked their evening meal, Danny went up to his room. He sounded confident that God would work things out for Mrs. Barber and Kirk and Karen, but now that he was alone he was vaguely disturbed. He knew that God answered prayer, that God knows when a sparrow falls and he sees that the lilies are clothed. Yet everything did look so hopeless, and for himself, too. If Mrs. Barber lost her home, he might have to find a new place to live—and a job, too.

Danny Orlis sat down at his desk and opened his history book, but the dates and names blurred. He could scarcely recall what he was reading. His thoughts came back again and again to Mrs. Barber and her troubles. Finally he pushed aside his history book and bowed his head and prayed.

# SEVEN
## *Answered prayer*

There was a committee meeting that evening. Danny
went a little early. It had been a couple of weeks since
he had talked to Kay alone, without some of the gang
around. But when he got there he saw that Marilyn
had come a little earlier. The shade was up and she
and Kay were sitting on the davenport in the Barnes'
living room.

"I'm glad you've come, Danny," Kay said when he
had sat down in the overstuffed chair across the
room. "Marilyn and I have just been talking."

"Fine," Danny said. "How are things going, Marilyn?"

"Not so good."

His brow furrowed. "That's not the way it ought to
be."

"It's because of her mother and dad," Kay put in
quickly. "You remember I was telling you that they
think she's too 'religious.'"

He nodded.

"I–I tried to talk with them about Jesus," Marilyn

said. Danny saw that her lips trembled. "I tried to re-member those verses that you read to me, Kay, and to tell them how a person has to be born again, but they can't understand. They look at me as if they think I'm crazy."

"That's tough," Danny said. "We've been praying that it would be easier for you."

"Daddy graduated from State university," Marilyn continued. "He says that no one who is intelligent and educated believes the Bible. He says that it's just a bunch of made-up stories; that Jesus isn't the Christ at all. He's just a great man, a man we all ought to try to follow, but not to worship."

Danny got up and walked across the room. "I'm not smart enough to argue about things like that," he told her. "But I know your dad isn't right. I know that every word of the Bible is God's Word and it is true. And I know that Jesus is the Son of God. We're com-manded to worship him."

"I know that, too," Marilyn said firmly.

"Whatever your dad or anyone else tries to tell you about the Bible, don't let them get you twisted up on things like that," Kay put in.

"Daddy is going to send for some books for me to read," Marilyn continued. "But I don't want to agree. I want to believe the Bible. But I don't know very much about what's in it, and I'm really afraid to read Daddy's books. They might—"

Just then the doorbell rang and Kay went to answer it.

"Kay and I will be praying for you every night, Mari-lyn," Danny said quickly.

"Please do."

During the committee meeting Marilyn was strangely quiet. When it was over she asked if Kay could walk home with her.

"Surely," Kay said. "I'll get my coat."

"I need someone like you to talk with," she said gratefully when they were out on the sidewalk. "I don't know which way to turn."

Kay said nothing.

"I thought I wasn't going to have any more troubles after I took Christ as my Savior. But that's all I've known since I became a Christian." She paused a moment. "I honestly don't know whether I'd have come out for the Lord if I had known what was going to happen at home. I'd have thought I could never have stood it."

"That's one thing we can know that God does," Kay said, her voice ringing with assurance. "He always gives us strength to overcome temptations that come our way. All we have to do is to be sure that we're putting our full trust in him and not in ourselves."

"It makes me feel stronger and more sure of myself to be with you, Kay. You seem to have the right answers."

When they reached the Forester home Marilyn stopped.

"I'd like to ask you in, Kay," she said. "I don't think I'd better the way things are." She fumbled uncertainly with her gloves. "Daddy does not like to have me with you and Rick and Danny anymore. He—he says that you're a bad influence."

Kay took her arm and gently squeezed it reassuringly.

"But you're the best friend I ever had," Marilyn

blurted out. Then, before Kay could answer, she turned and fled into the house.

Danny and Rick walked home silently from the committee meeting.

"Why don't we go to the ice cream shop and have a soda?" Rick asked.

The Orlis boy shook his head. "Can't. I've got a big history test coming up the first period in the morning, and I haven't finished studying."

"OK," Rick replied. "I'll see you in the morning."

He had planned on going directly to his room to study, but when Mrs. Barber heard him open the door she called to him.

"Come here Danny," she said. "I–I want you to meet the man who bought the house we live in."

Danny quickly hung up his coat and cap in the hall closet and went into the dining room.

"I think I met this young man," the tall stranger said, smiling. "I talked with him one day when you were out. I'm Keith Meyer." He held out his hand.

After the introduction they all sat down.

"Mr. Meyer has made arrangements to move here the first of the month."

"I see."

"That's one thing I wanted to talk to you about," Mr. Meyer said to Danny. "I think I told you about my boy, Kenneth. He'll be in your grade at school."

Young Danny nodded.

"I came over to make final arrangements about the house tonight," Mr. Meyer went on. "I came to talk to you, too. I've heard a lot about you since I've been nosing around Cedarton."

"I hope it's been good," Danny said seriously.

"It has been," Meyer replied. He took an expensive watch from his pocket and looked at it. "My boy, Ken, is a good boy. But I've been worried about him in the past few months, Danny. He drives too fast and doesn't study like he should and. . . . " He paused momentarily. "He's been in with the wrong crowd over at Edgerton. I thought perhaps if I'd come and talk to you, you might be able to get him in with the guys you hang around with."

"I'll do my best," Danny agreed. "Of course, he might not like the things we do."

"I think he'll like you," Mr. Meyer said, smiling. "That ought to help make him like the things you do."

"Maybe you can bring him around and introduce him." Danny suggested. "That is, after you get settled."

"I hardly think that will be necessary," the man continued. He smiled again. "That is, if Mrs. Barber is agreeable to what I have in mind."

"I don't understand," she began.

"I came over to see you tonight, too," he said to her. "Kenneth's mother died when he was just a little guy. We've had a regular parade of housekeepers. Some of them have been good, and some not so good. The boy needs a woman's hand, Mrs. Barber. I was just wondering if you and your youngsters and Danny would care to stay on here and let Ken and me move in. I'll pay for the work, of course."

For an instant or two Mrs. Barber sat staring in disbelief at tall silver-haired Mr. Meyer.

"Do you mean you—you want us to stay on here?" she asked incredulously.

"That's right," he repeated. "Of course, I want to bring my own furniture and do some remodeling but I would like for you to stay. We'll move in, Ken and I."

"B–But there's Kirk and Karen," she said hesitantly, "and Danny's been staying with us. That will make the house a little crowded."

Mr. Meyer smiled warmly.

"It's a big house," he said. Then he leaned forward. "Frankly, Mrs. Barber," he continued, "your family and Danny have been a deciding factor with me. Ken and I have lived alone too long. It's not good for my son. He's becoming selfish and spoiled. I'm very concerned about him. He needs to be around other boys his age. He needs something closer to a normal life than I've been able to give him."

Mrs. Barber straightened slowly. It was as though a weight had been lifted from her shoulders. The light came back into her eyes. "You'll never know how much this means," she said gratefully. "I've been nearly frantic with worry."

"It looks as if we're all happy, then," he said. "I'm delighted with the arrangement."

Then Mrs. Barber turned to Danny. "I should have known you were right," she said. "God does look after and take care of us if we just let him."

"That's right," Danny said. "He hears and answers prayer. We've got to put faith in him to work things out."

Mr. Meyer looked at him. "That's strange talk from a boy," he said. Something about his sharp look made Danny twist uncomfortably.

"I'm a Christian," Danny said simply.

Mr. Meyer looked from him to Mrs. Barber.

44

"That's the second time I've heard that remark in this house," he said. He reached for his hat.

"I just don't know how Ken's going to take that sort of thing," he continued, more to himself than to them. "You see, I've never believed in sending Ken to Sunday school or church."

"You mean you didn't want him to go?" Danny questioned.

"It isn't that," Mr. Meyer went on quickly. "But I believe in free expression. I want Ken to take his place in some religious organization sometime, but I do not want to influence him. I want him to grow up so that he can make up his own mind without prejudice."

Young Danny said nothing. Finally, during an awkward silence, Mr. Meyer got to his feet.

"I must be going," he said. Then he turned again to Danny. "I'd certainly appreciate it if you'll do what you can to help Ken. I'm terribly worried about him."

"I sure will," Danny Orlis answered fervently.

"Fine," Mr. Meyer said. "If I were you, though, I believe I would soft pedal the religious stuff. I'm afraid it would ruin everything. He doesn't have much use for it."

"I can't promise you that, Mr. Meyer."

When Ken's father had gone, Mrs. Barber came back into the living room and sank into a chair, her eyes brimming with tears. "Oh, Danny," she said, her voice choking, "it's all so wonderful, I can scarcely believe that it's true."

The next morning Danny met Kay on the way to school and told her what had happened.

45

"Oh, that's wonderful!" she exclaimed.

"I was so happy for Mrs. Barber I could hardly sleep last night," Danny said. "God certainly answered our prayers."

"I'm glad something good has happened," she said seriously.

"What do you mean?"

"It's Marilyn. I'm terribly worried about her. She's come so far in her faith, and so fast that you can scarcely believe she's the same girl."

"That's nothing to be so concerned about. That's good news."

"Her parents, Danny," she said. "She's testified before them and they're determined that she's not going to be 'religious' as they call it. They think she's queer and they don't want her to go with us or to Bible club or Young People's anymore."

"Boy, that's rough. What's she going to do?"

"They haven't actually forbidden her yet," Kay said, "but they've told her they'd rather she didn't have anything to do with fanatics. They're doing all that they can to get her back to the old crowd. Her mother even wanted to have a dance for her Sunday night."

Danny was silent for a while. "She's going to have a hard time," he said at last. "It's hard enough for those of us who have Christian parents who try to help us live clean, separated lives. I don't know about someone like Marilyn."

"We'll have to pray for her, Danny," Kay said. "We'll have to pray for her harder than we've done before."

# EIGHT
## *The know-it-all kid*

The Barber household was busier that week than they had ever been before. Mrs. Barber washed the windows, scrubbed the woodwork and floors, and packed her own things so there would be room for Mr. Meyer's furniture when it arrived. Danny got home as soon as he could after school and helped.

On Friday the big moving van pulled up to the front door, and two men began to unload the finest furniture Danny had ever seen in his life.

As he started toward the front door, tall, dark-haired Ken Meyer came in.

"Hi, Orlis," he said. "Remember me?"

"How could I forget you?" Danny said, putting out his hand. "You really clobbered us."

"When I played hockey against you I never thought we'd be living together."

"Neither did I," Danny replied.

"Thought I'd get over here and pick out my room before my father got here and beat me to it," Ken said. "Come up and show me around." It wasn't a request. It was an order.

"I thought I'd give the movers a hand," Danny replied.

"Let them do it," Ken said airily. "That's what they're paid for." He took Danny by the arm and the two of them went upstairs. "I want a room with a private bath," he said, "and one that's got plenty of heat."

"We can fix you up with the heat all right," Danny answered as he laughed, "but I'm afraid you'll have to share the bath with the rest of us. There's only one bath on each floor."

"Well," Ken said, "you people can use the one downstairs."

Kenneth Meyer poked into all five of the upstairs bedrooms, nosing into the closets and squinting darkly at the windows. "Some dump," he snorted. "What's got into the old man, buying a place like this?"

"We've liked it a lot," Danny said. "It's a nice house."

"Well, there's only one decent room up here," the new owner's son announced. "I'm going to have that."

At the dinner table that night, however, Ken learned that he wasn't getting his way with either the room or the bath.

"I don't care if you do like Danny's room," Mr. Meyer informed him with a strange firmness in his voice. "You're not going to have it. And as far as turning the upstairs bath to you is concerned, it's so ridiculous that I'm not even going to answer you."

Ken sputtered but looked at his father's set jaw and said nothing more.

When they had finished eating, the newcomer

pushed back from the table and got to his feet.

"Come on, Danny," he said. "Let's take the car out for a spin and see what this burg is like."

"I'm sorry, Ken," Mr. Meyer said, "but I'm going to be using the car tonight."

"What?" he echoed disdainfully.

"I'm going to be using the car," his dad repeated.

Ken's lips curled in contempt. "What are you trying to do?" he demanded. "Get tough?"

"That's enough, Kenneth," Mr. Meyer snapped, his voice rising.

"OK," the boy snarled. "If that's the way it is, OK. I can get along without the lousy car." He started toward the door. "Are you going with me, Danny?"

Danny started to refuse, but he looked over at Mr. Meyer and saw the unspoken plea in the man's eyes. "Sure," the Orlis boy said. "I'll go."

By this time Kirk had finished. "I'd like to go along, Danny," he said. "Can I?"

"I don't see why not," Danny answered.

"What do we have to do, baby-sit with him?" Ken demanded.

"Don't worry about Kirk," Danny said. "He can take care of himself."

The three of them put on their jackets and started out the door and down the steps.

"Come on, Flash," Kirk called to his big shaggy shepherd dog. "Come on, old boy."

"Flash," Ken taunted. "That's some name for a dog like that. How come you call him Flash?"

"Because if you throw a stick he'll go get it in a flash," Kirk announced proudly. "He's the best dog in Cedarton. Aren't you, boy?"

The dog seemed to understand him because he came closer and licked at Kirk's mittened hand.

"We'll try him out some day," Ken said. "We'll try him and see just how good he is."

They walked up the long street and across the park toward the lake. Danny tried to talk to Ken but was not very successful. They walked most of the way in silence.

"I guess the ice skating's over for another year," the Orlis boy said.

"Oh, it is up here," Ken Meyer said offhandedly. "But I always go down to the Cities a couple of times a month to keep my hand in for hockey. A guy can't be a good skater and just do his skating in the winter time."

They walked down beside the lake and stood there looking out over the ice.

Ken reached down and picked up a piece of wood someone had used to build a fire.

"Let's see how good that dog of yours really is, Kirk," he said.

"Don't, Ken," Kirk cried. "Don't throw it out on the ice. That ice is awful soft. It—"

He reached for Ken's arm, but the taller boy eluded him and heaved the stick far out on the ice.

"Fetch, Flash!" he cried. "Fetch!"

With a bound the dog dashed out onto the ice.

"Flash!" Kirk cried. "Flash, come back!"

But it was too late. The ice cracked and creaked!

"Flash!" Kirk shouted in dismay. "Flash!" He started to run as fast as he could toward the dog.

"Kirk!" Danny cried. "Come back here!" But the wiry boy eluded him.

Kirk Barber dashed out onto the ice, shouting to his dog. "Flash!" he called. "Flash! Come back! You'll drown! Come back!"

At the same time there was a thin, brittle crackle of ice followed by a splash and a frightened yelp of the dog.

"Flash!" the boy cried.

Danny had recovered his surprise by this time and started running toward the boy. "Come back here, Kirk!"

But he wasn't fast enough. Ken forged ahead of him out onto the soft, slush ice and grabbed Kirk by the arm.

"Come back here," he panted. "You'll drown!"

"But my dog!" Kirk sobbed, trying to tear away. "I've got to get my dog!"

"I'll get your dog," Ken told him. "Come on back here off this ice before we all break through."

Reluctantly Kirk allowed himself to be guided to the safety of the shore. Flash was barking and whining plaintively as he swam in the freezing cold water.

"What about Flash, Danny?" he pleaded. "He'll drown."

"We'll do our best to get him, Kirk," the Orlis boy told him, "but it's going to be tough. That ice is awfully soft and thin."

He turned to talk to Ken, but the tall, angular newcomer had already run through the snow to a pile of rough lumber a hundred yards or so away.

"What are you doing, Ken?" Danny called. "Aren't you going to help get the dog?"

His companion didn't answer. Instead he jerked a long two inch board off the pile and began to drag it

51

toward the lake. Danny saw what he was doing and went to help him.

"Leave it alone," Ken panted. "I got Flash into this. I'll get him out."

"But you've got to have help!" Danny protested. "You can't go out on that ice alone!"

"If I want help, I'll ask for it," Ken snapped. "Now leave me alone." With that he moved cautiously out on the thin ice, shuffling his feet through the slush that the warm, late March sun had created.

"Do you think Ken can get him?" Kirk asked Danny, his lip trembling. "Do you think he can?"

"We'll have to pray that he does," Danny muttered. "And that he gets back safely, too."

Ken Meyer moved cautiously with the careful skill of one who is well acquainted with the ice and all its treachery. He edged forward a dozen steps or so, then placed the board on the ice and scooted on it toward the place where Flash was floundering. He moved so slowly that it seemed he would never get there, and yet the space between them narrowed until a scant yard separated him from the tiring animal.

He lay down on the plank and stretched out until his fingers were within inches of the dog's cold, wet fur. He slid forward until his fingers touched Flash's collar. There was a faint, warning snap of cracking ice and Danny sucked in his breath sharply. But the long plank held Ken from breaking through. For what seemed five minutes or so to Danny—but was probably only a few seconds—the boy on the ice paused, summoning strength. Then he began to pull slowly and steadily on Flash's collar until he had the big, trembling dog up on the ice again.

"He got him, Danny!" Kirk cried. "He got him! He got him!"

"Now then, Flash," Ken said in a voice that was different than Danny had ever heard him use before. "You stay with me, and I'll get you back on safe ice again."

Without turning around, Ken scooted backward until he was over shallow water where he knew the ice was still firm.

"You got him for me, Ken," Kirk cried, kneeling and throwing his arms about the cold, wet dog. "You got him for me! Thanks! Thanks a lot!"

"You did a real good job," Danny said admiringly. "That ice is mighty tricky this time of year."

Ken looked at him for a moment or two, queerly, then his face twisted into a grin. "It's nothing if you know how," he said. "It just takes somebody who knows what he's doing!"

"You can say that again. Kirk and I were sure praying for you."

"Praying for me?" Ken echoed sarcastically. "That's a laugh!"

"I don't know why it should be," Danny said. "We always look to God when we need help."

Ken Meyer laughed.

"So you pray," he said. "That's something. No wonder you were scared to go out on the ice, if that's the kind of a guy you are."

"I wasn't scared," Danny started to protest. Then he stopped short. What good would it do to argue with him? It would only antagonize him and make it harder to talk with him.

"Well," Ken said, starting off alone. "I think I'll be

getting uptown before you start preaching to me. So long."

"Thanks for rescuing Flash for me," Kirk said gratefully.

"Aren't you going to put the plank back where you got it?" Danny asked.

"Why should I?" the newcomer asked offhandedly. "They can find it if they look for it."

When he was gone, Kirk sighed deeply. "Boy, he's brave," he said. "I don't think I ever did see anyone that brave."

Danny nodded. He went and got the plank and dragged it back to the pile. Ken was brave all right, and smart. He was so self-sufficient he would be terribly hard to talk to about the Lord. Together, Danny and Kirk walked toward their home with the shivering dog trotting by their side.

# NINE
## *The joyride*

At the Forester home across town, Marilyn helped
her mother with the dishes after a late evening meal
and sat down in the living room with her English literature books. Her father had gone back to the office.

"It's good to see you sitting down with lessons for a
change, Marilyn," her mother said, picking up a thick
novel and dropping into a heavy over-stuffed chair beside the fireplace.

"What do you mean?" Marilyn asked.

"It's just good to see you studying," Mrs. Forester
said pointedly, "instead of sitting around with your
nose in a Bible. It's more normal, I mean."

Marilyn laid aside her book.

"Mother," she said hesitantly, "you used to want me
to go to church and Sunday school. You used to get
me up and make me go whether I wanted to go or not.
Why did you change your mind all of a sudden?"

"It isn't that I don't want you to go, dear," her
mother countered. "For I do, and so does your father.

It isn't—isn't 'religion' that we object to, it's this fanatical religion. This reading the Bible all the time and learning Bible verses and missing out on all the fun in life. That's what we do not approve. We want your life to be balanced, like our lives and those of our friends."

"But I don't miss out on any fun," she replied. "I have more fun with Kay and Danny than I ever had with that other crowd. And I've never been happier. It's wonderful to trust the Lord, Mother."

Mrs. Forester sighed her resignation. "That's just the sort of thing I'm talking about," she said. She leaned forward and laid her hand on Marilyn's arm. "Your daddy and I have great plans for you, dear. We want to send you to the finishing school I attended and prepare you to take your place with the better people. Why, if you persist in this silly religion the way you've been the past few weeks, you'll be laughed right out of society."

"I don't know how to put it into words, Mother," Marilyn stammered, "but I know that I've found what I want more than anything else in the world."

"And what," Mrs. Forester smiled, "could that be?"

"The Lord Jesus Christ," Marilyn said simply. Her mother stared at her, shaking her head slowly. "I don't know what we're going to do with you, Marilyn Forester."

She started to rise, but Marilyn spoke desperately. "Mother," she pleaded, "I–I know you'd feel differently about all this if I could just explain it to you. But I don't know so very much about the Bible."

"You should," her mother snapped. "You've got your nose stuck in it half of the time."

"Mother," Marilyn repeated, "could I have Kay come over and talk with you? Could I?"

"Now who is Kay?" Mrs. Forester asked scornfully. "Is she one of that Bible bunch you've been running with?"

"Oh, you'd love Kay. She's the sweetest girl I ever knew. Her mother's a missionary down in Mexico, and her dad was killed there. You'd just love her. And she could explain all these things that I can't. Would you talk with her, Mother?"

Mrs. Forester got to her feet. Her face had flushed crimson and her eyes were snapping. "I want to tell you this, young lady," she announced angrily, "you're not bringing this Kay person or anyone else over to try to convert me." She turned on her heel and went into her bedroom and slammed the door.

Marilyn sat there for a long while staring at the closed door, her eyes brimming with tears.

Danny took Ken to school with him the next morning and introduced him to the guys. Neither of them mentioned what had happened the night before.

After supper that evening, Danny excused himself from the table and started upstairs.

"Where are you going, Danny?" Ken asked.

"To get ready for Young People's at church tonight," the Orlis boy said. He stopped and came back into the living room. "We're having a special speaker. Want to come along?"

Ken thought a moment. "It doesn't sound like much fun to me."

"Oh, but it is," Danny told him. "We have a fine time over there. There's about twenty-five or thirty now. I know you'd like it."

Ken shook his head. "Not tonight," he said. "I think I'll wait until I get a little better acquainted here."

"It sounds like a good place for you to get acquainted," Mr. Meyer put in. "Why don't you go?"

"Nothing doing," his son countered. "There's probably only a bunch of drips there anyway. I'll tell you what I will do, Danny. I'll give you a lift over there in the car."

"Great. We'll stop and pick up Rick."

They stopped for Rick, and Ken stepped on the gas and headed for the highway.

"This is the wrong way to the church," Danny protested.

"Church?" Ken laughed. "Who wants to go to church? We'll go over to Edgerton and have a lot of fun. I know a bunch of girls over there."

"But we don't want to go to Edgerton," Rick put in.

"Oh, you don't?" Ken echoed. "Well, now, that's too bad." He screeched around the corner, the motor roaring, and slammed the pedal to the floor.

"Ken!" Danny shouted. "You're going seventy-five!"

"Who cares?" he grinned. "This crate will do a hundred ten."

At that moment a piercing wail of a police siren sounded behind them.

"The highway patrol!" Danny exclaimed.

Ken Meyer's face went white at the first sound of the siren. His forehead became beaded with sweat. His hand trembled uncertainly on the wheel, and the car lurched in the loose gravel before he righted it.

"It's the highway patrol," Danny repeated. "We've got to stop."

Ken still maintained his speed, though the piercing whine of the siren grew closer and closer. "I can't stop," he told them, his lips quivering. "They picked me up in Edgerton for speeding a couple of months ago. This time I'll lose my driver's license. I can't let them catch me!"

"We've got to stop!" Rick put in firmly. "It'll only make matters worse to try to run away."

Ken's voice turned to pleading. "You get under the wheel, Danny," he begged. "They'll let you off easy the first time. Maybe they'll just warn you. You get under the wheel for me. I—I'll pay the fine and everything."

The Orlis boy shook his head. "Nothing doing," he replied firmly.

"How about you, Rick?" Ken asked. "I—I'll make it worth your while. I'll do anything you want me to, only get under this wheel."

"Not me," Rick said.

"Fine pals you are," young Meyer snapped. "I'll outrun 'em. That's what I'll do."

He jammed the accelerator to the floorboard as the patrol car began to draw up alongside. The big eight-cylinder car started to draw away, but Danny reached down, turned off the ignition and removed the key.

Ken swore angrily as the car swerved to a stop with the highway patrol car alongside.

"What's the big idea, Orlis?" he muttered under his breath. "Now we are in for it."

"Not half as much as if we'd tried to run away from them," Rick told him.

The patrolman came storming back to the car.

"Just where do you think you're going at seventy-five miles an hour on a gravel road after dark?" he demanded.

Ken did not answer him.

"Let's see your driver's license," the officer ordered. He took one look at Ken's driver's license and whistled in amazement. "You've been a busy little fellow, haven't you? The judge is going to be interested in this. The chances are that he'll give you a rest from driving for a while."

"You—you aren't going to give me a ticket, are you?" Ken asked hesitantly.

"I wouldn't be worthy of wearing this badge if I didn't," the patrolman said. "We'll be seeing you in court a week from tomorrow morning. Bring your dad along."

"Y—yes sir," Ken answered.

The officer turned to Danny and Rick. "Do either of you fellows have a driver's license?" he asked.

"I do," Rick said.

"All right," the officer opened the car door on the driver's side. "Come around here and drive this car back to town. And don't drive it over forty or I'll slap a reckless driving charge on you, too."

"My dad doesn't like to have anybody else except me drive the car," Ken protested.

"He can't be so very particular," the officer snapped, "or he wouldn't be letting you drive." With that he turned and strode back to the patrol car.

For several minutes the three boys sat staring into the darkness.

"Boy, that's tough, Ken," Danny said. "I'm awfully sorry."

"And it's all your fault," Ken accused, his voice rising in anger. "You wouldn't help me by getting under the wheel. Then when I wanted to outrun the guy, you shut the motor off. Now I'll lose my driver's license for six months, or a year, maybe. It's all your fault!"

Rick started the car and drove slowly back into Cedarton. Ken crouched against the door in the far corner and sulked. Nobody said anything.

"Where do you want to go, Ken?" Rick asked.

"What difference does it make?" he said bitterly. "After tonight, I won't get to drive the car again."

"I think maybe we'd better go home, Rick," Danny said softly.

"OK," the driver replied. "I guess we don't feel much like going any place."

Rick drove into the garage and shut off the motor.

Ken got out of the car and started across the lawn to the back door. There he stopped nervously and turned back.

"Say, guys, would you do something for me?"

"That depends," Rick answered.

"Would you go into the house with me," he asked, "while I—while I tell Dad what happened tonight?"

"Of course," Danny said quickly.

The three of them entered the house reluctantly and went into the living room where Mr. Meyer was sitting reading the paper.

"Well, now," he said, looking up. "I didn't expect you boys home so soon. Your meeting isn't out yet, is it?"

There was a long silence.

"We didn't go to the meeting," the Orlis boy told him.

"You must not have gone any place else, either," he continued. "I never did know Ken to get in much before midnight when he had the car."

Ken shuffled nervously from one foot to the other. "Dad," he said at last. "We—I mean I–I got to driving a little too fast on the Edgerton road and—" He stopped and swallowed hard.

"You didn't have a wreck, did you?" Mr. Meyer asked quickly.

"Oh, no," Ken said, "nothing like that. The highway patrol stopped us, that's all."

Mr. Meyer laid aside his paper. "So the highway patrol stopped you," he said icily. "Did they give you a ticket for speeding?"

Ken nodded miserably.

His dad got slowly to his feet. "Come on up to my room, Ken," he said. "I want to talk to you alone."

# TEN
## *A risky chance*

Danny and Rick sat in the living room for a few
minutes talking. Neither of them felt like going to
Young People's after what had happened. Finally
Rick decided to go.

"I've got some studying that I've got to do. I'll see
you in the morning, Danny."

After letting his friend out, Danny started upstairs
to his room, only to meet Mr. Meyer coming down.
The gray-haired man's face was grave.

"Danny," he said. "I want you to know that I don't
blame you or your friend at all for what happened.
I've been having trouble like this with Ken ever since
he got old enough to drive."

Danny said nothing.

"I'm terribly worried about him," Ken's father went
on. "I've thought maybe you could influence him by
getting him in with a different bunch of kids than he
was running with at Edgerton. I'm beginning to
believe even that wouldn't make so much difference.
He needs a little 'religion.'"

"It isn't religion that he needs, Mr. Meyer," Danny corrected respectfully. "He's just like you and me and everyone else. He needs the Lord Jesus as his personal Savior."

A perplexed look came across Mr. Meyer's face as though he did not exactly understand what Danny was saying. Then he took a deep breath. "I'd give anything in this world," he said, "if Ken were like you. You'll do what you can to help him, won't you, Danny?"

"Of course I will, Mr. Meyer," the young Orlis boy replied.

Danny went on upstairs and knocked on Ken's door. There was no answer.

Danny knocked again and again. After a long silence Ken called, "Who is it?"

"It's me, Danny."

"Just a minute till I unlock the door."

The Orlis boy stepped into the room and dropped heavily into a chair.

"Boy, I sure made a mess of things," Ken said bitterly. "The old man's so mad he'll never let me drive even if I don't lose my driver's license. And if I get fined I've got to get a job and work until I get it paid off."

"Your dad only wants you to respect the law, and get you to doing what he asks you to do."

"I sure messed things up," Ken went on as though he didn't hear Danny. "I didn't plan on speeding. I didn't plan to do anything. I don't know what's the matter with me."

Danny crossed his legs. "I do," he said.

"It wasn't enough to get the old man to lecture,"

Ken bristled. "I suppose now I'm going to have to listen to you spout off."

"Take it easy," Danny said. "I'm not going to lecture. I just said that I know what's the matter with you, and I do."

"OK," Ken grunted, "out with it."

"Well," Danny began, "my dad always says that every one of our problems has a spiritual answer. That especially applies to guys our age, Ken. We want to run our own lives in our own way. We want to do what we want to do, when we want to, and we don't want anyone telling us anything. Nobody can live like that. There are the laws of the country and there are the laws of God."

Ken sighed deeply but said nothing.

"But more important," Danny went on, "there's the Lord Jesus. If we really recognize that we are sinners and our lives are in a 'mess' as you say, and if we confess our sins and put our trust in Jesus, he'll straighten everything out for us."

Ken Meyer sat there for a long while staring at Danny. "What kind of stuff are you trying to feed me?" he asked. He tried to sound flippant and hard, but somehow the sincerity of his question showed through.

"It's the truth, Ken," Danny said. "All we have to do is turn to the Bible." He got out his Testament and opened it to verses that told of sin and man's need of a Savior. He read of the promise of eternal life for all who confessed their sins and put their trust in Christ.

"I could never live that way," Ken protested earnestly. "There wouldn't be any use for me to try. I could never live good enough to be a Christian."

"That's just it," Danny continued. "You can't do it, and neither can I. If we could, salvation wouldn't be by faith. We'd have to work to earn it. We've got to put our trust in Jesus and depend on him to help us live as we ought."

Ken got up and crossed to the dresser. "I'd have too much to give up," he said uncertainly. "I don't think I could do it, Danny."

For a moment or two Ken Meyer eyed Danny intently. Then he walked to the bed and sat down, biting his lower lip as though to keep it from trembling.

"You don't want to keep putting it off, Ken," Danny said slowly. "Don't you think you're ready to take Christ as your Savior?"

There was a long silence. Ken took his pen from his pocket and examined it. Danny got out his Testament and began to thumb the pages.

"I can't see it, Danny," Ken replied. "A guy's got to give up so much to become a Christian. I want too much out of life. I know I couldn't do it, Danny."

"But you don't give up things," Danny protested. "Not really. It's just a matter of putting first things first, and substituting the things God wants us to do for the things we want to do."

"But I have so much fun," Ken objected. "And I'm going to keep on having it."

"You don't really know what fun is," Danny said, "until you put your trust in Christ. Honestly, Ken, I wish you could see the gang at Young People's and Bible club. You never saw a bunch of kids have more fun."

"It's not for me," Ken snapped. He got up and

walked to the dresser. "That's not my kind of fun."

"It doesn't cost the price your kind of fun does, either," young Orlis countered.

"What do you mean by that?"

"I couldn't help thinking of that fast ride you gave us, and the trial that's coming up."

Ken Meyers face was sober. "I get into one mess after another," he said. "I don't know what's the matter with me."

"I've been trying to tell you," Danny persisted. "It's because you won't let God rule your life, Ken. That's all that's the matter with you."

"Stop preaching! You can't force me to become a Christian! I'm going to do it! You can depend on that. But I'm not going to do it until I am good and ready! I'm going to have my fun first."

Danny started to answer him. He started to argue about the foolishness of putting off something as serious as accepting Christ, even for an hour, but he could tell by Ken's manner that it wouldn't do any good. He arose. "Well," he said, "I've got some studying to do. I guess I'll be getting to my room."

The resentment faded from Ken's eyes. "I'm sorry about talking to you that way, Danny," he said. "I didn't mean to get angry, but I'm not ready to become a Christian."

"Dad always says that this is the thing a guy can't possibly afford to postpone. If you're planning to take Christ as your Savior, you'd better do it tonight, Ken. It's dangerous to put it off."

"I'll take my chances," the other boy said. "I'm not ready yet."

The next morning Danny planned on walking to

school with Ken. He might get to talk to him again. But Ken got up, dressed, and slipped out the front door to school while Mrs. Barber was preparing breakfast. At school he avoided Danny's steady, friendly gaze whenever he could.

The story of Ken's wild driving and the chase by the highway patrol man mushroomed as it traveled through the school. Between classes and at noon a gang of boys flocked about him admiringly.

"Were you really going a hundred and ten, Ken?" Butch Winston asked.

He shook his head. "Nope, I had those dopes, Rick and Danny along. They started to squeal when I got her up to eighty-five." For an instant he forgot the trial he was facing under the glow of their frank admiration. "If it hadn't been for them I'd have outrun the cops easily. The old man's car is really souped up. It'll get out and go."

"Boy," Butch sighed. "I wish I'd have been with you. Will you give me a ride some day?"

"If I ever get my driver's license back," Ken laughed.

Danny and Rick walked on. "It sort of makes you sick, doesn't it?" Rick asked, "to hear him talk like that after what happened."

"He's just talking. He doesn't really feel that way inside. He's miserable. And the worst is he wants to put off taking Christ as his Savior."

"Did you talk with him?"

"For a long while last night. He acted as though he was under conviction, but he wouldn't give in."

"If he doesn't now," Rick said, "before the trial, he might never do it."

"That's what I'm afraid of," Danny said slowly.

# ELEVEN
## *The trial*

In another part of the school, Kay and Marilyn were getting on their coats.

"Are you going to be able to go to the committee meeting next week?" Kay asked.

"I don't know," Marilyn said, hesitantly. "I'm going to try."

"I sure hope you can." They walked down the steps and out onto the sidewalk. "It's at Danny's, and it's one of the most important committee meetings of the year. We're going to plan all the programs we'll be having between now and the time school is out."

"If I miss it," Marilyn answered, "it won't be because I want to."

They walked for a half a block or so. Kay turned toward her friend. "How are things going?" she asked finally.

Her companion shook her head and for a brief instant tears filled her eyes. "We—we just don't talk about spiritual things anymore," she said. "Daddy thinks it's terrible that I even try to live as a Christian should, or that I believe the Bible. He's ashamed of me, Kay."

"Have you ever tried to testify to him, Marilyn?" Kay asked. "Have you ever tried to explain to him what you believe and why, and tell him how happy you've been since you've taken Christ?"

"I—I've wanted to," she said, "but somehow I can't do it, I just freeze up when I think of talking to him about the Lord. I don't know why."

Kay was silent for a time. "Maybe that's what's wrong," she said at last. "Maybe if you'd explain everything to him he'd understand. And maybe you could lead him to Christ."

"Do you think I could?" Marilyn asked eagerly.

"It's surely something for us to pray about," Kay replied.

Marilyn stopped for an instant on the sidewalk in front of her home. "You know, Kay," she said seriously, "Christian kids who have got consecrated Christian parents don't know how fortunate they really are."

Ken Meyer's trial was called for the following Tuesday morning at 10:30. About an hour earlier Mr. Meyer drove out to the school and got Rick and Danny.

"What do they want us for?" Rick asked nervously.

"The judge will want to hear your story of what happened," Mr. Meyer said.

Ken was already sitting in the backseat of the car. His forehead was moist with sweat.

"Hi," Danny said as he crawled in beside him.

Ken had been bragging about his appearance

before the judge only the afternoon before, but now
his shoulders were twitching nervously, and his reddened eyes gave evidence that he had slept only a
little the night before.

"Danny," he whispered. "You won't tell them I was
speeding, will you? You won't tell them."

Young Orlis shook his head. "I'll have to," he said.

"Please, Danny." There was desperation in his voice.
"Please."

"I've got to tell the truth," Danny answered. "I'd like
to be able to say that you weren't speeding, Ken, but I
have to tell the truth."

"A fine pal," Ken snapped. "Believe me, I'll certainly
remember this."

The judge didn't take Rick and Danny's testimony
after all, for Ken pleaded guilty. The highway patrolman testified that he had followed the Meyer car for
a mile and clocked him at an average of seventy-three
miles an hour and the officer who had been riding
with him verified it.

"And to make things worse," the first officer said,
"he was driving on loose gravel on a road that had
very sharp turns."

"This is a serious offense, Kenneth," the judge
began, sternly. "And it's all the more serious when we
look at your record. You have one reckless driving conviction, two red lights and two speeding counts
against you. Isn't that right?"

The boy's face became crimson.

"I think, Kenneth," he concluded, "that you have for-
feited your privilege to drive. I'm going to suspend
your driver's license for a period of six months and
fine you seventy-five dollars and costs." He turned to

Mr. Meyer. "And I hope, sir, that you insist upon his paying every cent of the fine himself."

"You needn't worry about that, your honor," the boy's father said firmly. "I fully intend to see that he gets a job and pays the fine in full."

Marilyn had been praying a great deal for her father and that she would have the opportunity to talk to him about the Lord, but somehow the chance didn't materialize. For one thing, he was busier than ever at the office and seemed to be irritable.

When he came home at night he ate hurriedly and either went back to the office or out to the country club. For the time he had almost forgotten that Marilyn had become a Christian, or so it seemed. He said nothing to her about going to church or about her choice of friends. In fact, he said very little to her.

On the evening of Ken's trial, Marilyn's mother had a dinner engagement at the club and Marilyn prepared the evening meal for herself and her father.

"Well, now," Mr. Forester said, coming into the kitchen as Marilyn was putting the last of the dinner on the table. "It looks as though we're going to have a real meal tonight. Is this a demonstration?"

"I hope so," she said a little uncertainly. "I didn't realize that there were so many things to think about in preparing a meal. We'll have to wait a few minutes for the tea."

He laughed pleasantly.

They sat down at the table together. Mr. Forester reached for the bread.

"Daddy," she ventured timidly. "Don't you think it would be nice to ask the blessing?"

He looked at her. "I thought you were getting off that 'religion' stuff by this time, Marilyn. You surely don't expect to go through life living the way you've been living the past few weeks, believing that stuff!"

"Daddy," she said. "It isn't just 'religion' with me. Being a Christian is a whole way of life. And I'd like to have you share it with me. I'd like to have you become a Christian too."

"Huh," he laughed derisively. "I gave up fairy tales when I got my first pair of long pants."

"But Daddy," she pleaded desperately. "If you don't take Jesus as your Savior, you'll be lost and—and I want you to go to heaven!"

Mr. Forester's face turned pale and he shoved back from the table. "I never thought I'd be taking that sort of thing from my own daughter," he exclaimed. With a curse he got to his feet and stormed out of the room.

She stared after him for a moment or two. Then she buried her head in her arms and began to sob.

# TWELVE
## *Speed demon*

How long Marilyn sat there with her head buried in her arms she did not know. The grandfather clock in the living room struck seven o'clock and then seven-thirty. The dinner she had worked so hard to prepare had long since grown cold.

Once or twice her father stepped quietly to the kitchen door and peeked in, but she did not see him. Finally he came into the kitchen and pulled up a chair beside her.

"Marilyn," he said gently.

She raised her head slowly, reluctantly, and wiped at her swollen, reddened eyes.

"I'm sorry I didn't eat dinner after you went to all that work preparing it."

"That's all right," she answered quietly.

"I'd like to talk to you for a couple of minutes, honey."

"All right." She pushed back her chair and faced him.

"I know how you feel about this religion business,

Marilyn," he began. "I know you've been fed a lot of stories about Christ and sin and the Bible being true until you're so mixed up that you don't know what to believe."

"But I do know what I believe, Daddy," she told him, her voice trembling. "I know that everyone who has not taken Christ as his Savior is lost," she went on. "And I know that I've put my trust in the Lord Jesus and I'm going to heaven."

"When you get a little older and a little better educated you won't be talking such things," he said, smiling confidently. "You'll learn that religion has its place in life, but that it isn't all. You'll find out that Christ is the great teacher, the outstanding example, and that the Bible is a remarkable piece of literature considering the age in which it was written. But you'll learn that that's as far as truly educated people go."

He paused a moment, as though expecting his daughter to say something. Instead, she sat there silently, looking at him.

"Don't you see, Marilyn? It isn't that I'm upset about all of this. It's for your own good that I want you to be realistic. I haven't said much to you because I thought that this was a phase, a fad that would wear off in a week or two, but I'm becoming concerned now. I don't want you to waste your life so everyone who is somebody will laugh at you. I want you to be happy."

"But I am happy, Daddy," she protested. "I'm happier than I've ever been."

"Nonsense!"

"It's true," she continued. "Before, I was dissatisfied

and had to be doing something all the time, going out with the kids to a show or a dance. Sort of like you and Mother with the country club and your parties. Now I'm completely happy to—"

"That's enough!" Mr. Forester cut in. He got to his feet and took half a step toward her. "I've stood for a lot, Marilyn, but I'm not going to let you criticize your mother and me."

"I'm sorry," she said quietly. "I didn't mean to be disrespectful."

"You didn't sound like it." He started out of the kitchen, then turned and came back. "I've put up with all this clap-trap that I'm going to, young lady."

"W–w–what do you mean?" she asked.

"I mean that you're through with that church where they put such ideas in your head," he announced firmly. "And no more Bible club or running with that fanatical bunch."

"But Daddy—" she protested desperately.

"You heard me!" With that he whirled and stomped out of the room and upstairs.

Ken didn't go to school the afternoon following his trial, but the next morning he walked to school with Danny.

"I thought maybe if you were with me, Danny, the guys might not pester me so much trying to find out what happened at the trial," he said as they walked down the steps together. "I don't feel much like talking today."

The Orlis boy nodded sympathetically.

They walked to the end of the block, cut diagonally across the street, and waited for Rick on the corner.

"Dad really meant it when he said I had to get a job and pay that fine," Ken continued. "Have you got any idea where I could find something to do?"

Danny shook his head. "Boy, I had a rough time last September," he said, "when I tried to find work."

"I don't know what I'm going to find," Ken Meyer said, "but I've got to get something that'll make good money, quick. That fine and court costs amounted to over a hundred dollars."

Danny picked up a stone and skipped it along the sidewalk. "Tell me, Ken," he said, "Have you been doing any more thinking about the matter we were talking about the other night?"

A queer expression spread over his companion's face. "I don't know," he began, "what you're talking about."

"Have you decided to become a Christian?" the Orlis boy asked. "Have you decided to come through for the Lord?"

Ken shook his head. "I'm going to someday," he said, "but I'm not ready yet."

Danny eyed him intently. "Why wait?" he asked. "If you know that's what you want to do finally?"

"I want to have some fun first."

Rick came up just then, and Ken began to talk rapidly as the three of them headed toward school.

That afternoon after classes, Ken went out to look for a job while Danny and Rick walked slowly home together. The warm April sun was smiling brightly at the green grass and leafing trees. The boys took off their jackets and carried them loosely.

"Boy," Danny said. "I'd sure like to be up on the Angle now that the fishing season is open. The walleyes will really be striking."

"There's some good fishing in Cedar Lake right here in town," Rick said, "if we can just get a boat to go out after them."

"Maybe Ken will loan us his," Danny replied. "He's always talking about the great boat and motor he has over in Edgerton."

"As soon as he brings it over you ask him about it," Rick said. "I know some good fishing spots."

Danny meant to bring up the matter of the boat that night, but Ken himself mentioned it after supper.

"I got it, Danny!" he said jubilantly when they were alone together in Danny's room. "I got a job that will let me get the old man paid back in no time and still get enough money to buy gas for my boat."

"Say now," Danny answered, "that's fine!"

"Yes, sir," Ken went on. "All I have to do is wash and grease cars down at the Ajax Quick Service on Saturdays and Sundays."

The smile left Danny's face.

"What's the matter. Were you counting on that job or something?"

"No," Danny said, shaking his head. "It's just that you'll be working on Sundays, that's all. I was in hopes you'd get a job that would let you go to Sunday school and church with us."

"Still after my soul, aren't you?"

"That's right," young Orlis said seriously. "You need the Lord Jesus, Ken. We all do."

"I'm going to do it someday, Danny," Ken Meyer replied. "Just give me time."

Danny started to say more, but Ken got up and headed for the door.

"I've got to go down and see if I can talk the old man

into sending after my boat and motor tomorrow," he said.

"Rick and I were just talking about your boat," Danny said. "We've been sort of anxious to go fishing. He says there's some real northern pike and walleye right here in Cedar Lake."

"I don't know about the fishing," Ken replied, "but I know this. I'll give you a ride you won't soon forget. I've got a racing shell and a four cylinder outboard that'll go like a scared cat."

A few minutes later he stuck his head back in the door. "Everything's OK. We're sending after the boat tomorrow afternoon."

The next night after school Danny and Rick helped Ken get his boat down to the lake.

"I don't see how you can fish from this thing," Rick said, looking at the stubby, flat bottomed shell with its trim deck and tiny cockpit.

"Who said anything about fishing?" Ken asked, grinning. "I've got the thing for speed. Believe me it'll go. I'm going to enter some races this summer."

"It'll go, all right," Danny said, noting the step on the bottom to lift it out of the water. "Have you ever timed it for a mile?"

"No," Ken replied, "but we'll do that as soon as I get the motor tuned up. It's been sitting around all winter. I'll have to do some work on it before we take it out and try it."

It was several days before Ken got the motor tuned to suit him. He set it in a big barrel out in the garage and adjusted the points and carburetor, until it purred beautifully.

"There," he said at last. "Now we're ready to give you a ride that is a ride." He shut off the motor and loosened it from the barrel.

"You know, the last time I used this motor I about scared a guy to death. He was sitting out on the lake fishing as though no one else was within a thousand miles. Maybe he was asleep. Anyway, I buzzed him pretty close going wide open, and I thought he was going to jump out of his skin. Never saw anything so funny."

They got the motor down to the lake by pulling it in Kirk's wagon. Danny and Ken carried it out and fastened it to the racing shell.

"There are a lot of people out on the lake this afternoon," Danny said as he and Kirk got into the little craft and Rick shoved them away from the dock.

"Don't worry, I'm not going to run anyone down today. Boy, you don't trust me much, do you?"

Danny did not answer.

Ken gave the starter rope a jerk and the powerful motor leaped to life with a roar. The little boat skimmed across the smooth water.

Danny grinned broadly. This was really fun.

"How do you like it?" Ken asked.

"Fine," Danny shouted to him, "It's great!"

"Now I'll open her up," Ken said. He shoved the throttle over and the tiny craft seemed to sprout wings. The wind was whipping in their faces as they headed toward the open water.

And then Danny saw the slow, cumbersome fishing boat directly in their path. "Ken, we're going to hit him! We're going—"

# THIRTEEN
## *The terrorist*

The racing shell with Danny and Ken aboard bore
down fast on the helpless fishing boat, sending in its
wake long, deep rollers across the placid water in an
ever widening V. Danny shouted again.

"Ken! There's a boat up there! Look out!"

Ken Meyer laughed and held to his course as Danny
braced himself for the crash. "Don't get so excited.
I've got everything under control."

"Look out!" Danny shouted.

At the last possible instant, when the fisherman in
the flat-bottomed little boat in front of them was
white with terror, Ken shoved the motor hard to the
right. The big prop dug sideways into the water. The
speeding craft came around and skimmed past the
fishing boat with a scant foot to spare. A second later
the wake hit the fishing skiff, tossing it dangerously
and spilling water over the low side.

"Did you see him?" Ken chortled. "Boy, did he think
he was headed for the bottom of the lake! His heart
will be skipping beats for a week." He made a big,

swooping curve at half throttle. "Let's go back and get him from this side. We'll really give him a thrill."

Ken reached back to open the throttle, but Danny laid his hand on his in protest.

"I don't like this kind of stuff, Ken," he said, "it's terribly dangerous to come that close to another boat."

"I wasn't going to hit him," Ken said. "I was just going to scare him a little."

"If something had gone wrong with your motor you couldn't have kept from hitting him," Danny countered. "That's terribly dangerous."

"Listen, I know what this boat can do. We'll just buzz him again. I'll miss him by two feet if it will make you feel any better."

"Take me in first."

"What's the matter, fella, are you scared?"

"Yes, I'm scared," Danny answered firmly. "Anybody with any sense would be."

"I thought you were raised on the Lake of the Woods," Ken chided. "I didn't think a ride on this little mill pond would scare you."

"Sometimes we have to take chances up where I live," Danny told him, "when we're caught out on a lake in a storm or something. But I don't intend to take any chances I don't have to."

"All right, if that's the way it is, we'll go in; but I'll tell you one thing: You're the biggest chicken I ever met. No wonder the guys all make fun of you."

Ken would have gone out alone to scare the elderly fisherman again, but when he found out that Danny and Rick would go home without him he changed his mind. He had to get that heavy motor off the racing shell and pull it back to the house in the wagon. He needed help with it.

"I'll get Rick to come out with me tomorrow," Ken said, laughing. "I'll bet he isn't afraid to ride with me."

"Guess again," Rick said seriously. "I'm not riding with you or anyone else in that rig."

"That was just a sample tonight. Just wait until the next time. I'll really give you a demonstration."

"You needn't bother," Danny told him. "A sample is enough for me."

Together the boys got the big motor off and into the coaster wagon. The fisherman that Ken had buzzed a few moments before had started to row toward them as soon as they headed for shore. By now he was within shouting distance.

"I want to talk to you, young man!" he called. "You in the red sweater. I want to talk to you!"

"He means you, Ken," Rick said.

"If he thinks I'm going to stand around here," Ken said, grabbing the coaster wagon handle and starting to pull through the soft sand up to the road. "If he thinks I'm going to wait until he gets here so he can give me fits, he's got another guess coming. He's just mad because I scared him a little. That's all that's the matter with him."

"I'm going to wait for him," Danny said. "I'm not going to run away from him."

"Sure," Ken growled. "Wait around so you can tell him who I am and get me in trouble with the old man. Go ahead. See if I care." With that he half ran to the curve in the tree-lined road that would screen him from the lake.

"Where'd that other young fellow go?" the elderly fisherman demanded as he got out of his boat and pulled it up on the beach.

"He didn't seem to want to talk to you," Danny replied.

"I should think not!" the stranger stormed. "You saw him! He almost ran me down!"

Danny nodded.

"He'll kill himself or somebody else," the fisherman went on, "if he doesn't stop that foolishness." He stepped closer, brandishing a cane. "I wanted to give him a piece of my mind. And I wanted to tell you, young man, that you used good judgment in talking him out of buzzing me again, or whatever you call it, and in making him take you in."

"How did you know that?"

"You were both shouting above the roar of that motor, lad. Couldn't help hearing you." He stood for a moment or two staring up the road. Then he turned and stomped back down to his boat, leaning heavily on his cane.

"Look how crippled he is," Rick said quietly. "If Ken would have capsized his boat the old fellow would have drowned probably. He wouldn't be able to swim, would he?"

# FOURTEEN
## *A fatal mistake*

The next night the committee meeting for the Young People's Society was to be held at the Meyer home. Danny went home from school and helped Mrs. Barber straighten up the house and finish the dessert.

They were finishing washing the supper dishes when the doorbell rang and Danny went to answer it.

"Hi, Marilyn. I'll take your coat."

"I was just wondering," she said uncertainly, "if Ken is going to be here?"

"He'll probably be around the house someplace," Danny replied, "but he doesn't go to Young People's, you know."

"I know," she said. Her voice was dull and lifeless.

Young Danny eyed her. He started to ask her what was troubling her, but the doorbell rang again.

"Hello, Kay," he said, taking the newly arrived guest's coat. "Why don't you go into the living room while I run upstairs with this. Marilyn's in there."

"Marilyn?" she echoed. "Did she come?"

"Why shouldn't she?" he said. "You didn't happen to

forget that she's the chairman of the program committee, did you?"

"No," Kay said. "I didn't forget. Only . . ." Her voice trailed away.

When Danny came back to the living room Marilyn was saying, "No, Daddy didn't change his mind about my running with you kids, but—but—" she gulped hard. "He doesn't know where I am tonight."

"What?" Kay demanded.

"I mean he doesn't know why I'm here," she went on, flustered. "I told him it was a committee meeting and all that, and that it was to be over here at Ken Meyer's, but I didn't tell him it was Young People's."

Kay was silent for a long while.

"I didn't actually lie to him," Marilyn defended, quickly. "I didn't tell him that you kids would be here."

"I know," Kay answered slowly, "but I was just wondering. Don't you think you led him to believe that it was something different? That sort of thing can be almost the same as telling an untruth."

"I hadn't thought about that," Marilyn said. She twisted her handkerchief into a tight little knot. "But I just can't stand not being with all of you," she went on. "I've got to be with Christian friends, Kay. I've got to."

"I know how you feel," Kay answered.

There was a short silence. "You think I ought to have told Daddy the truth about the kind of meeting I was coming to," Marilyn said, "don't you, Kay?"

"It doesn't make any difference what I think, Marilyn," Kay said gently. "The thing that really counts is, what would the Lord Jesus think?"

"I'd never thought of it in that way." Marilyn got to her feet and started toward the stairs. "I'm going back home," she said, her voice choking.

Danny just shook his head.

The committee meeting went off as planned, but somehow Danny and Kay didn't have their hearts in it. They kept thinking of Marilyn, kept wondering what had happened when she got home.

Kay made it a point to see her in the hall between classes at school the next morning. "What did your dad say last night?" she asked.

"He just looked at me for a minute," Marilyn told her. "And then he said, 'so that's what all this being Christian amounts to.'"

"I'm so sorry," Kay said. "I had thought that maybe when he saw that what you do makes enough difference to you that you'd confess when you did wrong, it would make him see that it is something to be a Christian."

"So did I," Marilyn said, "but Kay, I don't think anything will ever bring him around—or Mother either. If I'm going to live for Christ, I've got to fight all the battles alone! The folks have never treated me this way before!"

The next few days were busy ones at school. The freshmen had their class party, the sophomores had a dinner in the basement of one of the churches, and the juniors had their annual picnic at the lake.

The rest of the class went directly to the park after school, but Ken went home first and half an hour later came pulling the wagon with his big outboard motor in it.

89

"Hi, Ken," Rick called. "I thought you weren't coming. Glad you changed your mind."

"Come on and give me a hand with this," he said, laughing, "and I'll give you a ride."

Danny and Rick went to help him. "We'll help you get the motor on the boat, but I don't care to take you up on the ride," Danny told him.

"Neither do I."

"Just wait," the newcomer said. "I'll give everybody out here a thrill. Just wait until I get this motor warmed up!"

"Take it easy," Danny warned. "Look at the people out here this afternoon!"

For an answer, Ken stepped lightly into his racing skiff and shoved away from the dock. The kids had all gathered along the beach by this time, watching as he started the motor and went roaring off.

"Look at that thing go!" one of the boys exclaimed admiringly. "Just look at her!"

Ken ran at top throttle a quarter of a mile or so out into the lake, then swept wide to come back parallel to the shoreline without cutting his speed.

"He's going to head for the dock," Danny half whispered. "Better get the kids off!"

But there wasn't time. The light craft skipped over the water with a deafening roar.

Too late, the kids on the long, narrow dock saw what he was doing. Frantically, they shoved toward shore. Ken was grinning broadly as the boat neared. At the last instant he shoved hard on the motor. The racing shell started to turn! But Ken had misjudged his distance! With a splintering crash the craft slammed into the end of the dock!

The light racing shell, skimming like a bullet on the water, seemed to explode as it hit the heavy dock. Kids were knocked into the cold water and the thin mahogany plywood splintered under the force of the blow. Ken was catapulted out of the cockpit and into the lake beyond the drop-off.

For an instant nobody noticed him. Everyone was shouting and screaming at once as they floundered through the cold, shallow water toward shore. Danny and Rick stood there, as though the accident had rooted them to the spot! The dock listed precariously, and the once proud little boat began to sink into the water.

Suddenly Danny straightened.

"Ken!" he shouted. "Ken!" He raced frantically toward the dock, tearing off his jacket and shirt.

"Call the emergency unit, Rick!" he shouted. "Quick!"

With that Danny dove into the water and swam rapidly toward the spot where Ken had gone down.

"Call the emergency unit, Kay!" Rick ordered, dashing toward a rowboat that had been pulled up on the beach. "Got to help Danny!"

"But how do I call them?" she cried.

"Come on," Marilyn said, "I know how!"

The two girls dashed across the park toward the nearest house while Rick rowed out to where Danny was swimming. No one else seemed to know what to do.

With long, powerful strokes Danny swam out to the place where Ken had been thrown into the water. His heart was hammering a tattoo as he dove for him the third time. The water was as clear as it was cold, but there was no sign of Ken.

"What if—" Danny stopped, forcing the thought from his mind. He had to find Ken! He just had to!

With a prayer in his heart he came up for air and went down again. He swam as he used to swim in underwater races back home at the Angle. Then his heart leaped. There was Ken, moving slowly, motionlessly, toward the surface.

With a half a dozen strokes Danny reached him and surfaced with him.

"Here, Danny!" Rick shouted when he saw them. "I'm over here with the boat!" But Danny did not hear him, and Rick had to row until his oar almost touched Danny.

Danny took hold of the back of the boat gratefully. His breath was coming in long, tearing gasps and his arms and legs were trembling.

"Hurry, Rick," he panted. "Hurry! Hurry!"

As they neared the shore, four or five of their classmates clambered into the water and carried Ken up on shore. For a moment or two Danny just clung to the back of the boat, too weary to move.

# FIFTEEN
## *Between life and death*

Rick had already started giving Ken artificial respiration slowly and methodically. The crowd waited tensely.

Danny finally managed to crawl out and stagger over to where Ken was lying, face down, on the beach.

"Is he coming around?" he asked.

Rick looked up and shook his head.

"Not yet," he said softly, scarcely mouthing the words. "I sure hope that emergency unit gets here."

Almost as he spoke they heard the siren whine and the white ambulance whirled into the park and came roaring toward them.

"What's the matter?" one of the men shouted as the truck stopped and he came running up to the high school students. "What's wrong?"

He saw Ken lying motionless on the ground with Rick working over him.

"Get the pulmotor, quick!" he called to the man in the ambulance. He turned to Rick. "Here, son," he said. "Let's get this machine on him as quickly as we can!"

With quiet efficiency the men worked over Ken. Rick stood there a moment or two, biting his lips, then he turned and walked to where Danny was lying.

"Are you all right?" he asked.

Danny nodded. He was trembling now and his face was blue with cold. Rick took off his coat and threw it over him.

By this time the doctor, who had been alerted by the same operator who called the emergency unit, came up. He got out of his car and strode over to Ken. Even as he got there the unconscious boy moved restlessly.

"He's coming around," one of the men said, his voice almost a whisper. "He's coming around."

A little murmur ran through the crowd. Danny got to his feet quickly, pressing as close to the unconscious boy as he could. Rick looked over and grinned. Danny nodded. Suddenly he felt warm again.

The doctor knelt beside Ken and examined him. "Yes," he said shortly. "He's coming around all right. His color's good and his breathing is almost normal."

"That's good," one of the men sighed.

"We've got to get him to the hospital as quickly as we can," the doctor went on. "Four of you come over and lift him exactly as I tell you."

"What's the matter with him, Doc?" someone asked.

"Not sure," the physician replied, "but it looks like a broken neck."

A breathless hush gripped everyone standing about. Danny caught his breath sharply. A broken neck! That must have happened when Ken was slammed into the water. Everyone had been so frantic about getting the water out of his lungs and getting them to working normally that they hadn't thought how they had handled Ken. Danny remembered, with a start, how queerly Ken's head had hung as his friends had carried him from the water.

They put Ken into the emergency unit with the doctor directing every move of the men who lifted him. Then one of the first aid crew drove the doctor's car while he got into the back of the ambulance and rode with his patient. Danny stood there numbly, staring after the slow-moving ambulance.

Kay came over to where Danny and Rick were standing. "Did—" she began hesitantly. "Were you ever able to talk to him at all about the Lord Jesus?" she asked.

Danny's eyes met hers. "He said he was going to come through for Christ some time," he told her, "but he kept saying that he wanted to have his fun first. He wasn't ready to be a Christian yet."

Tears came to her eyes. She turned away without saying anymore.

Danny and Rick went home after the authorities arrived to question them and others about what had happened.

"I almost hate to go home," Danny said.

"If we could only have made him see his need of a Savior. You know, Danny, he—he might die without having another chance."

Danny nodded grimly.

He was afraid that he would have to be the one to tell Mr. Meyer, but the doctor had already called Ken's father.

"They called about twenty minutes ago," Mrs. Barber said anxiously, "and Mr. Meyer went right down. We haven't heard since."

"He's pretty bad," Danny told her. "The fact is, he's awful bad."

He went up to his room and changed his clothes.

"Danny," Kirk said, sticking his head in the door. "We've been praying and praying for Ken to be all right."

"That's fine, fella," Danny answered.

"I was just wondering," Kirk went on, "is Ken a Christian?"

"That's the worst of it," Danny said sorrowfully. "He isn't, Kirk. He said he was going to be sometime but he just wasn't ready."

When Marilyn reached home breathlessly and told her parents what had happened, her dad got up and started for the hall closet to get his hat.

"Where are you going, Harold?" her mother asked.

"Down to the hospital to be with Keith Meyer," he said. "The poor fellow doesn't have a relative in town to help him carry this."

Ken's father was standing in the corridor of the Cedarton Memorial Hospital when Mr. Forester approached him. His lean face was ashen, his eyes dull and with a haunted expression. The two men shook hands.

"How is he?" Harold Forester asked.

Meyer shook his head. "Not good," he said. "Not good at all."

They sat for a few moments and talked, talked about things that didn't matter to either of them. Their thoughts were on the other side of that tightly closed door.

Finally Mr. Meyer looked up at his companion. "You know, it's a funny thing, Harold," he said numbly, "but I was always convinced that the way to make Ken strong and self reliant was to let him express himself, to let him find out things experimentally, to let him grow up without restraint."

"You can't blame yourself for what happened," Mr. Forester said. "This was just an accident. It doesn't prove that you were wrong."

"I've known for a long time that I've been **wrong**," he continued, "but at first I was too stubborn to admit it and could do something about it. When I finally woke up, it was too late."

A nurse came out of Ken's room closing the door behind her. She swept past them down the hall. Mr. Meyer stopped suddenly and stared after her.

Finally he spoke. "I was even so determined that Ken was going to grow up without my ideas and ideals being implanted in him," he went on, "that I deliberately kept him from Sunday school and church."

"I'm having my own troubles along that line," Mr. Forester said. "Marilyn's got to running with a bunch of fanatics out at school and came home one night telling my wife and me that she had 'been saved' and a lot of other foolishness. She took to sitting around the house reading her Bible when she wasn't studying. She got to praying before she ate, and telling Carrie and me that we ought to be saved too. We had to put a stop to it."

"You mean you really wanted to stop it?" Mr. Meyer asked, as though he could scarcely believe what he had heard. "Do you know," he went on after a moment or two, "that I would have given anything in the world if Ken would do that. That would have solved my problems, Harold. Ken wouldn't be where he is now if he'd listened to Danny and the rest of that gang."

There was a long silence. Then he continued, "Now I'm afraid it's too late!"

The doctor came along with the nurse two paces behind him. Mr. Meyer grasped her by the arm.

"How is he?" he asked softly.

She did not answer.

"How is he?" Mr. Meyer repeated.

She looked up, her eyes showing tears. "He—he's gone," she said quietly.

For an instant his fingers tightened savagely on her arm, then his grip loosened.

"I knew it," he whispered. "I knew it."

# SIXTEEN
## *Going home*

After the funeral two days later, the pallbearers' car stopped before the church and let the boys out. For an instant or two the guys stood, not saying much. Then, leaving Danny and Rick alone, the others went up the street.

"What are you going to do, Danny?" Rick asked.

"I don't know," he said. "Thought maybe I'd go home and change my clothes."

"Let's go down to the ice cream shop and have a soda," his companion suggested.

"I don't feel like eating," Danny replied. "Besides, the gang will be there. I don't want to talk to anyone this afternoon. I think I'd better go on back to my room."

"Come on," he persisted, "we can get a booth by ourselves. I don't feel like going home just yet."

"OK. I guess there isn't anything that should make me in such a hurry."

They walked down the narrow sidewalk to the ice cream shop where all the young folk went. Neither of them talked much until they reached the business district.

"Boy, it's going to be lonesome without you here this summer," Rick said. "Why don't you get a job around here and stay in town?"

"Oh, I couldn't do that," Danny said. "I've got to get back home." They crossed the street and went into the ice cream shop, heading for an empty booth. "But maybe you could come up and visit me. I could really show you some fishing up on the Angle."

They were just sitting down when Kay and Marilyn entered.

"Hi," Rick called to them. "Come, and have a dish of ice cream. Danny's got twenty cents."

"You didn't miss it far," Danny mumbled under his breath. "I think I've got a quarter."

Rick grinned at him. "This ought to be good," he whispered. "How are you at washing dishes?"

The girls came and joined them.

"We were just talking about the Northwest Angle where Danny lives," his friend said. "I'd sure like to go up there this summer."

"Oh, you'd love it," Kay put in. "I don't believe I've ever been to such a fascinating place. It's so quiet and peaceful and beautiful."

"Now wait a minute," Rick said. "You quit fishing for an invitation. Danny just asked me this summer."

"You know, I think we'd have room for all three of you," Danny said.

The waitress came and Kay ordered an extra thick malted milk. Rick looked up and winked at Danny.

"I–I think I'll have a root beer," Danny said. "A small one."

"You'd better give him a malted milk too," and Rick laughed.

Danny shook his head. "No," he said, "I think I'd better have the root beer."

"What's the matter?" Rick grinned. "Are you on a diet, or don't you like nice thick ninety-cent malts?"

Danny stared at him. "You know what's the matter, Richard Haines," he retorted, struggling to keep from laughing.

"What is this?" Kay demanded. "What's going on?"

Danny flushed. "Well, Rick knows I'm short of money," he explained. "He's trying to put me in a jam."

Kay's face crimsoned. "I didn't think, Danny," she said lamely. "I didn't mean to order that way."

"Oh, now, it's not as serious as all of that," Rick exclaimed. "I was just having a little fun. I've got five dollars from my uncle for my birthday, and I was planning to pick up the check."

"Oh," Danny said. "That's different. You'd better give me one of those strawberry malts too."

When the waitress had gone, Marilyn said soberly, "I can't get my mind off Ken. To think, he hadn't taken Christ as his Savior."

"I've been thinking the same thing," Danny replied.

Kay picked up a straw and broke it in two. "I know you and Rick tried your best to win Ken, Danny," she said, "but you know there's a lesson in this for us. There are many people just like Ken with whom we come in contact. It ought to be burned into our hearts that we should never pass up an opportunity to talk to them about the Lord Jesus. We never know when it's going to be too late."

"That's right," the boys said fervently.

When Danny entered the house half an hour or so later Mr. Meyer was sitting in the living room alone.

"Come and sit down, Danny," he said wearily. "I've been waiting for you. I want to talk to you."

Danny crossed the room and sat down in the big easy chair which Mr. Meyer usually used.

"I want to thank you for everything you did and tried to do, Danny," the sorrowing man went on. "You'll never know how much I appreciated it."

"I'm afraid I didn't do very much," Danny said uncomfortably.

"That isn't what I meant," Meyer replied. "I was talking about your efforts to make a Christian of him or whatever you call it."

"Rick and I both tried, Mr. Meyer," he replied. "Ken said he wanted to someday, but he wasn't ready."

"I know," the tall, gray-haired father said. "And it was my fault. I wasn't a Christian. I couldn't see why he should have any Christian teaching before he was old enough to decide whether he wanted it or not."

Danny said nothing.

"I've done a lot of thinking the past couple of days, though, Danny," he continued. "I began to see myself, a lost sinner, headed for hell."

"But you don't have to be, Mr. Meyer," Danny said. "If you take Christ as your Savior you can change all that."

For a brief instant a smile flickered on the man's lips. "I have changed all that, Danny," he said softly. "I went right from the cemetery to the pastor's study and there accepted Christ as my Savior."

"That's wonderful," Danny exclaimed.

Mr. Meyer was silent a long while. "I know it's

wonderful," he said at last. "But I can never forget that I condemned my own son to the very thing I've been saved from because I didn't guide him about his soul. That's something that will never heal, Danny."

Across town, Marilyn Forester was just entering her home after leaving the ice cream shop. Her father was sitting before the fireplace with the evening paper, still folded, on his lap.

"Is that you, Marilyn?" he called.

She entered the room. "Yes, Daddy," she said.

"I've been sitting here thinking about the Meyer boy," he said.

She sat down on a chair across from him.

"That was certainly too bad," he went on. "A young fellow like that, right in the beginning of life."

Marilyn nodded.

"I've been thinking about some of the things his father said to me the night I went up to the hospital," Mr. Forester went on. "He told me that Ken was awfully wild."

"Not wild, really," Marilyn countered. "He didn't drink, but he drove like crazy and didn't have any respect for his teachers or his dad or anyone else."

Her dad's forehead wrinkled thoughtfully.

"The thing that was wrong with Ken," she ventured timidly, "was that he did not take Christ as his Savior."

She had expected her dad to get angry at that, but instead he sat there staring at the carpet. "That's exactly what Meyer said," he replied at last. "He said he'd be alive and well today if he'd been a Christian like the kids you run around with."

"He probably would, Daddy," she said firmly.

Mr. Forester unfolded the paper and folded it again. "Is that Danny Orlis and Rick Haines and Kay whatever her name is, really like he said they were?" he asked.

"I don't know what he said about them," she answered, "but they're the finest bunch of kids I've ever known."

"Well," he said quickly. "I'm going to take back what I said. You can go around with them and to Bible club and to the church they go to if you wish."

She sat for a moment while the full realization of what he had meant swept over her. Then she said with delight, as she arose and went to him to kiss him tenderly, "Oh, Daddy!"

She straightened slowly. "Daddy," she said. "I must tell you that I had a malt with them in the ice cream shop this afternoon after the funeral. I haven't been running with them since you asked me not to, but Kay asked me to go down and have a malt and we ran into the boys."

"That's all right, honey," he said.

Danny had taken his last exam of the year and had his things packed ready to leave for the Angle when he went over to say good-bye to Kay.

"It's been so much fun going to the same school, hasn't it, Danny?" she asked.

"I'll say," he told her. "What time does your train leave?"

She picked up her ticket and looked at the envelope. "I've got about three hours," she answered.

"Tex is flying down after me in the morning," he

said. He walked over to the divan and sat down, "Do you think you'll be back here for school next fall?" he asked.

"I think so," she answered. "At least, that's what I'm planning on."

"I'd sort of like to go to a Christian high school," he said, "but I don't think I can scare up the money to do it."

"I'd like that too," Kay replied. "But I know Mother and I will do well to get me through here."

"I guess most Christian kids are in the same fix that we are," he continued. "I guess we ought to look at school here as a mission field and really do all we can to win the kids for Christ."

The phone rang just then and a moment later Kay's landlady came into the living room. "It's for you, Kay," she said. "I think it's Marilyn Forester."

Danny jumped to his feet. "Well, I'll be going," he said. "I'll see you in September."

"Write to me when you have time," she smiled warmly.

"OK."

Danny Orlis walked out into the brilliant spring sunlight. There was a bounce to his step and an observing passerby would have seen that his eyes sparkled. And why not? In the morning he was going back to the Angle. Home!